THE GIFT RARELY GIVEN

AMBAR CORDOVA

CONTENTS

DEDICATION

To those who believe in magic and love stories that feel a little unrealistic but that are a lot of fun… May your life this holiday season feel like a spicy Hallmark Movie. And if that fails, you'll always have Alex Haddock to remind you he can make all your dirty dreams come true.

… and to Caroline and Arlette, because Christmas is not the same without you. How unfortunate it is we are whole oceans apart. I hope every fun activity you do this December is a little less fun without me (just kidding. Las amo con todo).

AUTHOR'S NOTE

Hi friend,

I am so excited you picked up this Christmas novella. I hope you love it as much as I do, and that this story brings you joy this holiday season. There is so much I could say about this, but I just hope you give it a chance and that it is exactly what you're looking for. If you love it, feel free to message me on social media! I'd love to hear from you.

The Gift Rarely Given is a contemporary romance Christmas novella set in the beloved fictional town of Baker Oaks, Florida. It can be read as a complete stand-alone, but if you've read the rest of the Baker Oaks books, you might see some other beloved characters pop up. It is a novella, which means it's about half the length of a regular novel. It is meant to be a quick and fun story to read when life gets busy during the holidays.

I wanted to take a minute and acknowledge that, although there are many celebrations during the winter, this book particularly focuses on Christmas. I was the vessel in telling Alex and Livie's story, and theirs just happens to be Christmas-focused. It also has some on-page topics that may cause discomfort for the reader. I will list them at the bottom of this page, as they may be spoilers, and I want to allow those of you who may not be sensitive to skip them if they wish.

If you have read The Truth Never Spoken and The Trail Often Crossed and are wondering about the timeline, this story takes place the Christmas after Allie and Santiago arrive in Baker, but before they get their HEAs. There is, however, no crossover between the stories and it can be read as a complete stand-alone.

This book also includes a playlist and the closed-door option. You are welcome to skip until the following chapter when this symbol (⊟) shows up if you'd like to avoid the spice. The playlist is meant to be enjoyed per chapter but the book can totally be read without it.

Now for the content warnings. There might be spoilers, so if you want to skip this next part of the author's note, you can. There will be profanity, on-page descriptions of explicit sex, death of children (off page), hospital setting, children in hospice, diet culture toxicity, fatphobia, football injury (off page), and mental health struggles.

Thank you again for giving this book a chance.

143,

Ambar.

Playlist

PLAYLIST

THERE ARE no rules on how to listen to this playlist, but to enhance the experience, each chapter has a song title that matches the overall feel of that chapter. Feel free to listen to them after you read the chapter (or during if your brain will let you do that<3) Playlists are available on Spotify & Apple Music.

1. abdcefu - Gayle
2. Provenza - Karol G
3. Ho Hey - The Lumineers
4. Santa Baby -Eartha Kitt
5. Bubbly - Colbie Caillat
6. Use Somebody - Kings of Leon
7. Kid On Christmas - Pentatonix
8. I Don't Know About You - Chris Lane
9. This Town - Niall Horan
10. Feels Like - Gracie Abram
11. Call It What You Want - Taylor Swift
12. Dive Deep - Andrew Belle
13. All I Want For Christmas - Glee Cast
14. Winter Wonderland - Michael Bubblé
15. Weight - Alexz Johnson

16. The Door (Stripped) - Teddy Swims
17. Santa Tell Me - Adriana Grande
18. Marry You - Bruno Mars
19. A Nonsense Christmas

Scan for playlists

Spotify

Itunes

TWELVE DAYS BEFORE CHRISTMAS

On the twelfth day of Christmas, Baker Oaks gave to me a meet cute and a one-night stand with an elf and a grump.

1

───────────

TWELVE MINUTES
ABCDEFU, GAYLE

LIVIE

WHY THE HECK did I flip that guy off? Being frustrated is one thing but acting out that desperation and the rage is not like me. Walking through the busy sidewalks, I keep repeating the same scenario over and over again. Was I in the wrong? Did he somehow not see me with my blinking lights signaling I was waiting for that spot? On any other day, I would've let it slide, but I'm already running late. Running late to a date I don't want to go on, dressed like a Christmas elf, nonetheless.

My mother is on her quest to pair me up with yet another man she thinks will be the best suitor. The man who will put up with me and who will have me married with children by the time I'm thirty. She keeps setting me up for blind dates and I don't have it in my heart to let her know these men are not my type at all.

Tonight, I'm going to dinner and a ugly Christmas sweater party with Frank Johnson, the son of one of my father's business partners. I've met Frank before; the only reason I said yes was because Frank's mom saw me at the hospital and told me how excited she was at the prospect of having me date her son. The hospital I work for. I'm not even safe there.

Frank is obnoxiously polite with the personality of a potato. Not a potato. Potatoes are great. He's more like a ñame—a bland root vegetable my mom keeps making in different ways to try to get me to enjoy eating it since it has low calories. I love her, I truly do, but she needs to understand that life is more than getting married, having children, and keeping your weight at whatever number society has deemed acceptable.

I walk past the busy corner, making a right and rushing, trying to get to the door of The Salty Gator, where I'm supposed to meet Frank. By the time I get there, I'm going to be a puddle of sweat under this elf outfit. They said ugly Christmas sweater, I said *give me a whole outfit.* I couldn't find parking to begin with and to top it off, when I finally did, this asshat honked at me, as if it wasn't my parking spot he was trying to steal. I don't care that he was driving a gigantic SUV taller than all the other vehicles near me.

"Welcome to The Salty Gator! How many tonight?" the host asks as soon as I cross through the double doors leading to the main floor.

The smell of fried food and the joyful laughter welcomes me in and it helps me breathe easier. Relax, Livie, you can have a good time tonight. Maybe you'll like Frank. I try to convince myself before looking around and finding Frank, sitting on a corner table dressed with an elf shirt. *I guess I won't be the only elf here.*

"Thanks, but I'm actually meeting someone and I just spotted them" I reply politely. The host nods and allows me to head into the dining area. There's some sort of Christmas party happening tonight on Amelia Island but he wanted to do dinner first. Our moms got involved and now here I am, about to have dinner and then go to a party with this guy.

"Hey," I say as soon as I get to the table. Frank smiles at me but he doesn't even attempt to stand up.

"Olivia, welcome, grab a seat," he replies, grabbing his glass of wine and taking a sip. For someone who acts sophisticated all the time, I was surprised he picked this place. The Salty Gator is one of my favorite restaurants on Amelia Island but it doesn't necessarily scream 'fancy.' It's more like an upscale sports bar with delicious food and good drinks. The atmosphere is fantastic and you can't beat the marina and ocean view. Sometimes you can even see dolphins swimming and jumping, too.

"Livie, remember?" I say as politely as I can. Olivia is a family name so all the girls in my family are named that. My mom is Doña Via, my grandma Mamá Oli, my great grandma was Mamá Olivia and I don't like any of them, so Livie it is.

"Olivia suits you better. You're not a teenager anymore," he replies.

"But it's not what I like being called, so I would ask that you respect that." I grab my water cup and drink as much as I can before setting it back on the table. I snatch the menu and pretend to read it, knowing damn well I already know what I want. But I need a minute to settle or I will get up and leave this restaurant.

"Since you were late, I already ordered. I got us a couple of salads and the tuna nachos to share," he explains, grabbing his glass of wine and taking the smallest sip known to man.

Another thing I hate? Someone not letting me pick. I know it comes from deep within my soul, since my mother always has a say in what I should or should not eat. Which is why I like to order whatever I want, whenever I want it. Strike two Frank—one more and I will leave.

"Bummer, I really don't want a salad, so you can cancel it or take it to go," I reply, squinting at him so he knows I'm not playing games. I look around at the restaurant full of happy people. Some share fries at a table with those they love. Parents talk to their children. A group of men are watching the game while laughing. And I find myself completely irritated at the fact I'm sitting with Frank from HR.

The waitress arrives with the nachos. She sets them on the table and my mouth waters at the sight. Crispy wonton strips, a side of seaweed salad, queso and guacamole to dip, and seared ahi tuna on top. "Anything else I can get you guys?" the nice waitress asks, handing us both small plates and napkins.

"Two shots of tequila, please," I answer, handing her my menu. "I would also like to add fish tacos with sweet potato fries."

"Absolutely, is everything on them good?" she asks and I smile at her while nodding my head. "You got it. And for you, sir?"

"I'm good, thanks sweetheart," he replies and she rolls her eyes quickly enough that he won't see it but not fast enough for me not to notice and smirk.

We share the nachos in silence, the explosion of flavors dancing on my tongue. I close my eyes and almost moan. I'm so hungry I could eat a cow.

"So, Olivia, remind me what you do for a living?" Frank asks while wiping his mouth with the cloth napkin that should be resting on his lap. But he's obsessively wiping his mouth, cheeks, and fingers. I'm so distracted by the overuse of the napkin, that I forget I'm supposed to answer.

"I work with children in hospice," I answer, grabbing the shot that Layla, the waitress, brought and downing it as quickly as I can.

"Isn't it a waste of time if they're going to die either way?" he asks. The insensitive jerk. Strike three, Frank. There are so many reasons to hate going on blind dates. But going on blind dates organized by my mother—who is set in her ways about me marrying a man with money and class over anything else —is out of control.

"You know Frank, for someone with years of etiquette classes, you sure don't know how to hold a proper conversation with a woman—or with anyone, for that matter. There's no need for you to be a jerk, especially not about children," I snap, standing up and placing my white napkin on top of the plate with my barely-touched dinner.

"If you'll excuse me, I think this was enough for our dinner today. Clearly, we're too incompatible. I hope you have fun at the party." I grab my purse and turn around, walking toward the exit and leaving the restaurant as quickly as I can.

I grab my phone to text my best friend, Hailey.

> Me: 12 minutes

Hailey: That's a record. Did he smell?

> Me: No, he asked me if I worked with children who were going to die either way then why bother.

Hailey: Not the dying children.

> Me: FML, I'm so over this. I'd rather end my days alone than go on another painful date like that again.

I put my phone in my small snowflake-shaped purse and speed walk to my car, hoping to get out of there as soon as possible. It was a long day and, although Mr. Waffletwat said it so harshly, I do work with children who might not be here next year. Working in the hospice wing of Wolfgang Children's Hospital is not for the weak, but none of the children are, so I won't be either. If they can go through days and days of heartache and difficult surgeries with a smile, I can be there to hold their hand and give them strength. No matter how hard it is. I sure as hell won't let that stupid ass talk about them like they're not real humans who were dealt the absolute worst hand.

The air is cool this Friday evening and although I want to run for the hills, I walk toward the marina and find a bench right by the sidewalk. At least I can watch the sun setting without thinking about another failed date. *You will die alone, Olivia. I won't be here forever. You need a partner.* I hear my mom's voice in my head loud and clear. I may want a partner to share my life with but not at the cost of losing myself and my values in the process. I'm so tired. Tired of listening to my mom bitch about me not finding a partner. Tired of going on fruitless dates and tired of dealing with self-absorbed men. I tilt my head back and close my eyes, letting the breeze kiss my cheeks and hearing the roar of the waves as they take away all the memories from today.

2

THE MOST BEAUTIFUL
GIRL IN AN ELF COSTUME
PROVENZA, KAROL G

ALEX

WHO GOES to a tourist town the week before Christmas? Me, I guess. Why? Well because my friends are trying to get me to enjoy life again. Their words, not mine.

I drive around the narrow Centre Street full of cars parked on each side, watching people walking in and out of stores and crossing without a care in the world. Fuck. I hate Christmas. I hate the chaos, the lines, the overspending, and how commercial it all is. I hate that it is not even a season anymore, it's just Christmas and Santa, and elves and presents. It's not about family and time spent with others; it's about how much you can get or what others get that you didn't. Jealousy and frenzy surround everything—it's constant from Halloween until after Valentine's Day.

When I was a kid, this time of year was about magic and family time. It was about baking cookies, drinking hot cocoa or cider, and singing songs. It wasn't this craze of how much money we could spend to say sorry to our kids for missing out.

11

Or to show them love via toys. Or even worse, to gift them all the things we never could have when we were kids. I'm sure parents mean well, but really, shit's gotta stop. I even feel bad saying anything to anyone because I'm not a dad myself so I really shouldn't talk, but damn it. I'm tired of it.

I see a parking spot open on the far-end corner and hit my blinker, signaling I'm going in. As soon as I try to turn, this little blue Mazda2 zooms through like a bullet and parks. I hit the horn, and the driver just sticks their hand out and flips me off. I wait to see who had the fucking nuts to do something like that. I drive an Escalade and that little Mazda2 looks like a matchbox compared to my SUV.

The door opens and I'm expecting a raging dude, but instead, I get the most beautiful girl I have ever seen—in an elf costume. She's as short as her car, with curves that seem to go for miles. Her dress fits every inch of her. Her beautiful chestnut hair falls over her shoulders. She's shouting at me but I'm too dumbfounded by how stunning she is to even acknowledge anything. I hear a horn behind me, waking me up from my stupor, and before I know it, she has stomped away. She's walking fast down the sidewalk, disappearing into the sea of people holding bags of presents.

I continue to search for a parking spot, still thinking about the brief moment I saw her. I can't shake the feeling that I'm… smitten. What's wrong with me? Playing in the NFL for years, it wasn't unusual for me to be around pretty women. It was the opposite. I often had pretty women on my lap or in my bed. But there's something about this girl that shook me to my core. Maybe it was her pretty eyes or the sass she gave me over the parking spot she stole.

I drive around in the sea of vehicles, honking their horns in this chaotic maze where nobody has patience anymore. Everyone's restless, and with each corner I turn, hoping I'll find a spot seems unreal.

I'm about to call it quits and head back to the house when I see someone pulling out of their spot. I wait patiently as they leave, and then park my SUV. Stepping out, I head to The Salty Gator where I'm supposed to meet my friends.

Entering, I immediately notice how much cheerfulness is in the air. If outside was madness, this is sanity. Families share time and space. There's a group of friends laughing, music playing in the background, and a football game is on the TV. And at the back corner table is the cute little elf from earlier, sitting across from a man who looks like his idea of fun is getting drunk on champagne at events where everyone pretends to like each other but nobody truly does. He is also dressed like an elf, but where it suits her, he seems out of place.

"Alex!" I hear someone shout and I scan the dark-lit restaurant to find my friends Jake, Nick, Bobby, and Mason sitting at a high-top table facing the TV and the elf's table. I let the hostess know my friends are already there and walk toward the back until I reach their table.

"What's up, man!" Jake greets me, lifting his beer and pointing my way.

"Same shit, different smell," I reply, patting Nick on the back and nodding at the rest of the guys. We all played football in high school together, and somehow we're all back in Baker Oaks. Some by choice, some by life. Jake had an injury in high school that killed his career, so he never made it to college or pro ball. Nick played in college for a couple of years, but he stopped when his girl Natalie got pregnant with their daughter and he needed to work when he wasn't in school. They're still together and have one of the healthiest relationships I've seen. They're a breath of fresh air. Bobby, Mason, and I played our whole college career but I was the only one drafted.

Football was my heart and soul until two years ago when a

bad hit broke my femur. A couple of surgeries later, I was on the mend before an infection took over, benching me for longer than anticipated. After that, there was no going back. I have full mobility but not enough strength to go back and play. So, in the end, we're all just a bunch of ex-athletes with new lives ahead of us. At least they do; I'm still trying to figure out what the hell to do with mine.

I take a seat on the stool, my eyes straying to the pretty brunette in the corner. If she's on a date with him, it must be new because I can tell she's uncomfortable. Her shoulders are tense and her hands are closed fists at her sides. He looks at her when he talks but I can't tell how she's reacting since her back is to me.

"How was everyone's day?" I ask, trying to snap out of it by asking trivial questions. Before anyone responds, we hear a loud scraping noise; when we turn to look, we see the girl standing up, almost shouting at this guy. If I was closer, I could probably hear what she's saying but I can soon deduce that she's pissed and the conversation is over. She grabs a snowflake with a strap—a purse maybe?—and marches out of the restaurant.

I turn back to the table and find the guys preoccupied with the TV, not as interested in the disaster date unfolding near us. They make a few comments but I can't hear anything. All I can think about is figuring out who this girl is and what happened back there. I close my eyes and squeeze them tight before shaking it off and falling into conversation with my friends.

"ARE you going to the market tomorrow?" Nick asks as we stand on the corner of Center and First, waiting for the train to pass so we can cross to the parking lot.

"Christmas Market in Baker sounds like all my nightmares coming true, so that's a hard pass for me, dog."

"The girls would love to see you if you decide to get over your Scrooge spirit and come out."

I love Natalie and Bella, and if two people could talk me into going out on a day completely filled with holiday cheer—obnoxious holiday cheer—it's them.

"I'll try but I won't promise, so don't tell them anything."

"Good to see you, Alex. Call me tomorrow if you make it," Nick says and turns toward his SUV as I keep walking straight toward mine. The sun has set already but it's not deep into the night. The stars and the moon shine bright and, when combined with the streetlight, I can see the parking lot clearly and the marina beyond. I can also see a certain sassy-parking-spot-stealer-elf sleeping on the bench across from the water.

I make a split-second decision to go check on her. Amelia Island is usually safe, but that doesn't change the fact that she's a woman sleeping on a bench, at night, alone. I approach her as quietly as I can, being careful not to scare her. Because after all, I imagine I'm a tall and scary motherfucker if you don't know me.

A fact the press had no problem in reminding me and everyone who would listen. Stay away from Alex Haddock. Alex Haddock, womanizer on the street. Alex Haddock makes another scene at a bar. What the press doesn't know is that I haven't had a drink in years. I barely go anywhere, let alone bars, and I haven't been with a woman in a long time. It's hard to date anyone when everyone just remembers you as Haddock the Quarterback, not Alex the man. It gets old quickly, so I'm sure I'm destined to die alone.

She's sleeping on this bench completely at ease. She looks peaceful, without a care in the world. Almost like she had been helping Santa distribute toys and was too tired from working all day so she collapsed here. Her skin is covered in goosebumps, though, so I take off my hoodie and cover her.

She wiggles until she's comfortable and stills. There's not another bench for me to sit on but I find a big rock against a palm tree, giving me the perfect spot to sit down and keep an eye on her.

3

ARE YOU LIKE FAMOUS OR SOMETHING

HO HEY, THE LUMINEERS

ALEX

"GOOD MORNING, sunshine…or, should I say, elfie?" I ask as soon as I see her move and open her eyes. I know I scared her when she jolts at the sound of my voice, but I figured it would be best to just get it out of the way.

"Who the fuck are you?!" she shouts. "It's not even morning!" She sits up and drops my hoodie onto the ground.

"Your guardian angel, apparently," I reply, bending forward and picking up my jacket from the ground. "You fell asleep and it didn't seem safe to leave you here by yourself. I saw you while walking back to my SUV, but now that you're awake, have a good night." I get up to leave, but before heading to my SUV, I add, "You're welcome, by the way."

"Shit, I'm sorry. You didn't have to keep watch. I can't believe I fell asleep. What the hell?" she questions, still groggy from sleep and frantically looking for the snowflake pillow that I can see now is a purse.

She grabs the purse, opens it, and gets her phone out, checking it and letting out a curse. "Sorry; thank you for keeping an eye on me, but I'm good now." She stands up, shaking her dress out and stepping closer to me.

She offers me her small hand so I can shake it. I notice immediately how much I tower over her and that she's even prettier up close. Her long lashes kiss her cheeks, her skin a beautiful contrast with her dark hair and her freckles. And her body…her damn perfect body. All soft, sexy, and feminine curves. And when her eyes lock on mine, the sensation coursing through our fingertips intensifies. I pull my hand away and grunt.

"I'm glad you're good. I hope you make it to wherever you're going to dress like that safely," I say. I was trying to go for flirty and fun but it came out snarky as fuck.

"What? You've never seen holiday glee in human form before? That's sad, even for a grump," she sasses back.

"A grump? I'm not a grump. You're the grump, flipping me off when you stole my parking spot."

She gasps loudly, holding her hands together over her chest and dropping her mouth. "Your parking spot?! I was already there, and my blinker was on, and—wait, are you stalking me?"

I can't help but roll my eyes. "I was there first and, no, I'm not stalking you. It's hard to miss someone dressed like Cindy Lou Who on a Friday night," I tease. Fuck, why am I arguing with this girl instead of asking her out? "A cute Cindy Lou Who," I add, trying to smooth over this increasingly worse moment.

She rolls her eyes and folds her arms over her chest. "I was going to a party, hence the outfit, but now I just look ridiculous, I guess."

"Cute. You looked cute even when you stole my parking spot," I explain, winking at her and stretching my hand in front of her again. "Hi, I'm Alex, nice to meet you."

"Livie," she replies, shaking my hand softly.

"You hungry, Livie? I saw you didn't stay for your dinner date long earlier."

"So, you are stalking me," she teases with a smile. The air around us is crisp and her arms break out in goosebumps. This time I offer my hoodie to her, holding it between us in a silent gesture.

"I'm harmless, I promise. You were sitting across from my table back there—" I point to the restaurant—" and I saw how quickly you left, so unless you went to eat somewhere else, I bet you're starving."

I can see hesitation shifting in her eyes. "Are you asking me to go eat with you?"

I grin and reply, "I am." She looks at me, her gaze searching my eyes with her hands on hips. Her body language shows how confident she is in her own skin but her eyes are telling a different story. To her, I'm just a giant asshole creepy stalker. If she was my sister—if I had a sister—I wouldn't want her to go anywhere with me. "Listen, this was a bad idea. You don't know me, and for all you know I could be a serial killer, so just forget it."

"Well, are you?" she asks, and when I raise my eyebrows, she continues, "A serial killer?"

I grunt and pinch the bridge of my nose, shaking my head.

"Okay, how about this?" Livie continues. "We do dinner, but I pick the place and I'll drive myself. When the dinner's over, I go my way and you go yours. Deal?" Her lip curls in a questioning smirk as she waits for my reply.

"Say where."

She tells me the name of the restaurant—Yummy's, a mom-and-pop burger shack down the road. We hop into our vehicles and park one behind the other on a quiet side street near the diner. I wait for her to step out of her car and lock it before I fall into step behind her, keeping my distance so she doesn't assume I'm trying anything funny. Amelia Island has a small-town feel, despite the tourists. There are a lot of empty side streets that only locals know about, but we just met—I don't want to spook the girl.

I text my mom to let her know I won't be home early tonight before putting my phone back in my pocket. I might be thirty years old but I've lived with my mom since my injury, so even though I'm an adult, she still worries if I don't let her know where I am. As we reach the front, I pull open the glass door, letting Livie walk inside first and she whispers a soft thanks.

The bright white lights in the restaurant combined with the checkered floor scream retro diner. Livie hits the bell on the red countertop and we wait as we browse the menu lit-up above the register. This place is known for its burgers and milkshakes, and I can go for both of those. Good to know that this is where her mind went when I asked if she was hungry.

"Welcome to Yummy's. Can I have a name for your order?" the purple-haired cashier asks.

"Livie. Can I have a double cheeseburger with sweet potato fries, add salt and Yummy's sauce on the side, please?" she orders without hesitation. Her confidence in knowing what she wants is hot as fuck, too. I already knew she was confident—the outfit, the way she sassed back when I mentioned the parking spot, and the way she ended her date back at her restaurant—this was just the icing on the cake.

"You got it. Anything to drink?"

"Cookies and cream milkshake and a cup of water, please. Thank you." Livie reaches for her tiny purse but I quickly reach over her to hand the cashier my card.

"On me," I whisper to Livie, squeezing her shoulder softly and stepping next to her so I can put in my order.

"And for you, sir?" she asks, taking my card.

"Let me get a Reuben and a slaw dog. Tater tots, and a root beer." The cashier finishes inputting the order on her computer and then taps my card on the reader.

"Here you go. Take this number to any table and your food will be right up," she says.

"After you," I tell Livie, turning my body so I'm right behind her. And being the forward asshole I am, I put my hand on her lower back and guide her toward the sitting area.

She walks to a booth in the back corner, far away from the entrance and the rest of the people here. It's late but in December—when everyone's trying to buy presents, spend time with family, and do things out and about—the night's still young.

"You didn't have to pay," Livie protests, sliding into the booth.

"I asked you to come eat with me. I did need to pay. It also was not a problem at all."

"So, tell me, Alex. What brings you out on this busy December night, and why are you free so at this hour?" Livie asks, laying her elbows on the table and leaning closer while resting her hands under her chin.

"Dinner with my friends and, to be honest, I'm always free. I don't do much anymore."

"And why is that?" she asks with surprise in her eyes.

I smirk. "Why do you look surprised? Maybe I'm a loner and you were the only person who took the bait."

"Nah, looking like that—" she says waving her hand like she's roving my body"—and with the smooth talk, I don't think it's hard for you to spend time with anyone. On top of that, you appear to be a gentleman. So, what's the real reason?"

"How do you know I'm a gentleman, Livie?"

"Opening doors, hand on my lower back, paying for dinner, and watching over a total stranger as she sleeps on a bench in the dark? All gentlemanly things if you ask me."

"It's called the bare minimum, but sure, I guess I am. My mama raised me right."

Livie opens her mouth like she's ready to say something

else but the waitress brings us our drinks. She grabs a straw from the table, unwraps it in one quick swoop, and puts it in her milkshake. She closes her eyes, takes a long sip, and moans. I look at her full mouth as it's wrapped about the straw and all my blood goes south, even as I try to keep it from happening.

"She sure did. You're dodging the question though." She's all business like she didn't just look like the sexiest thing on earth while sipping on her drink.

"I don't get out for many reasons. Maybe I'll tell you about them next time. But I'll give you one now if you answer a question for me." I sip on my root beer, letting the bubbles fizzle and tickle my throat before asking, "Why did you abandon your date back there?"

She flashes me a giant smile and says, "Easy and simple. It was a date set up by my mother, and that guy has the personality of a ñame. He also ordered me a salad for dinner after I'd just gotten off a long day of work and had to deal with the parking nightmare that is this town. I couldn't take it. Your mama raised you to be a gentleman; mine raised me to give pleasantries, and today, I'm out of them."

"Fair. Also, what's a *yamay*? Is that what you said?"

"Hahahaha, kinda," she answers. "Ñame is like a potato without flavor."

I choke, trying not to spit out my drink at that description. After I swallow, I laugh. A deep laugh that registers between a cough and a cry. I don't remember the last time something made me laugh like this.

"It's the truth. Just another Chad, Brad, or Kyle that my mother tried to pair me with so I don't lose on my fertile years," Livie explains, adding air quotes to the last two words. "Sorry, natural over-sharer. Your turn."

I shake my head, still laughing a bit. "Don't be sorry at all. I'm sorry you were set up with someone like that; sounds to me like you need more personality."

"Than a root vegetable? Yes, please. I rather pluck my eyelashes out one at a time than deal with that for hours. My mother, on the other hand, doesn't get that. Still over-sharing here. I'll shut up now."

"Don't," I chuckle. "I could listen to you talk all night." I wait a few seconds in silence before looking her in the eyes, deciding to go for it. "I don't go out much because my life came to a standstill three years ago. It's only recently that I've been able to go anywhere without help. And let's just say… my reputation is a disaster and trying to fix it is not as easy as it seems. Everything I do gets picked apart by the media, so now I don't do anything at all." I usually don't have to talk about my career with women because they hunt me down for who I am. Alex Haddock, the ex-quarterback legend, not Alex the man.

"What are you, like, famous or something?" she asks, turning her face to the waitress as she brings us our food, dropping our plates in front of us and making the silence stretch longer. I hate this question almost as much as I hate getting recognized on the streets. There's never a good way to explain who I am, and even years after setting foot in that stadium for the last time, it doesn't get any better.

"Or something," I mutter.

"Mysterious. Well, enjoy your food." Livie grabs her cheeseburger and takes a big bite. She closes her eyes and moans again. She clearly enjoys food, and I like that. I really like that. Girls tend to be nervous while eating in front of a man. They're worried about looking a certain way or not ordering what they truly want in fear of what men might think. I, for one, don't give a shit. I'd much rather be on a date with someone who is trying to have a good time and be themselves than someone who is trying to impress me.

"You too," I reply, trying not to think about how I don't remember the last time I enjoyed an easy conversation with a girl while sharing a good dinner.

4

———

HAPPILY SATED

SANTA BABY, EARTHA KITT

LIVIE

WE FINISH our dinner mostly in silence. We talk about a few more trivial things, staying away from the heavier topics our conversation started with. I, a pathological word blurt queen, and Alex, trying to appease my interrogation. I do enjoy talking to him and sharing this dinner, which is new. I was starting to lose hope in the whole dating scene—not that this is a date, but if it was, it would be a ten out of ten.

I do like that this is not a date, though, because of the way he smells—like a cozy winter night stuck in a cabin somewhere, baking cinnamon cookies—and the way he looks. If this was a date, I wouldn't be wondering what would happen if I dragged him out of here to a quiet alley and let him have his way with me. But because this is not one, I do contemplate it. His hands are broad and strong, and when he touched my lower back all my senses came to life. I've never met someone so charged with masculine energy, nor has my body ever answered to it like this.

The chances of seeing Alex again are slim since I don't

25

live in this area. I'm about an hour away from home, and he only knows my name. I've seen the way his eyes have roamed all over my body a few times tonight, so I know he's interested. I can sense it. So…maybe I should just go for it and see where it leads.

We get up from the table, leaving a pile of plates and trash on top of a tray, ready for them to pick up since we couldn't find a trashcan to do it ourselves. As we leave, he opens the door for me, and we're out into the dark chilly night. I have lived in Florida my whole life, so when it's fifty degrees, it's freezing. I didn't grab a jacket because it didn't fit the costume and I regretted it all night. Not now, though. Because if I did indeed have a jacket, I wouldn't be able to feel Alex's hand, warm and heavy, on my lower back. I wouldn't be able to feel his warmth as he gets close to me, and I like it. A lot.

We walk down the street, making a left on the empty and dark road where we parked. Very smart of me to pick a street with little to no traffic. Perfect spot for getting mugged, but also —now that I think about it—it might be the perfect spot for a quick sexual escapade if I can gather the courage to propose it. Other than the hand on my lower back, there hasn't been any contact between us. Other than his roaming eyes, there hasn't been any indication that he's thinking about the same things. But I've been going crazy for the past hour and I need something.

I stand by my car, turning to face him. Alex keeps his distance, forever the gentleman, when all I want is for him to take a step forward, slam me against the car, and kiss me senseless.

"I guess this is good night," he murmurs, his eyes fixating on mine like he's looking for something.

"Do you know what I haven't had in a while?" I ask him, twirling a piece of my hair around my finger.

"What's that?" he asks, taking a step closer and showing that he can read the damn signals. A hot, easy to talk to, gentleman who's smart too. If this man is single because he doesn't know how to fuck, I'm going to be so pissed.

"A good night kiss," I whisper into the air, biting my lip and not dropping my gaze for one second.

"Oh yeah?" He presses closer, placing a hand on the window of my car and caging me in. His other hand caresses down my cheek until his fingers reach my neck and he holds me in place.

"I can rectify that." His deep voice rumbles over my lips before he closes the small gap between us, brushing his lips to mine.

As our lips touch, it's like a whisper, delicate and inviting. He gets comfortable exploring my mouth and slowly deepens the kiss. His hand tightens the grip he has on my neck, pulling me closer to him. I hum a quiet moan behind my lips and when I roll my hips against his pelvis, I notice how hard he is already. He lets out a guttural groan, deepening the kiss even more. Claiming my mouth as his own even if just for this moment.

He breaks the kiss and his breath is warm against my lips. The lingering taste of root beer on my tongue makes me crave one more taste. It's making me crave more of him. We stand there quietly panting in each other's arms.

"What a kiss," Alex whispers against my lips.

"It can be more," I reply, rolling my hips again and pulling another groan from him.

"Are you trying to kill me here, Liv?" I really like that this near-stranger of a man, who just gave me the best kiss of my life, just called me Liv. The one nickname I've wanted from a man my whole life and it came naturally out of him. Another brownie point for him.

"You drive a big SUV, Alex," I tease. "I bet there's plenty of room in that back seat of yours."

"You are…you are trying to kill me," he whispers against

my lips. "I don't want you to think this is why I asked you to have dinner with me."

"What if I want you to find me attractive enough that the only reason you asked me to dinner was so you could fuck me later?" I ask. I've gone my whole life not asking for what I want, and with the high chance of not ever seeing him again, what is there to lose?

Alex shakes his head. "If you walk around thinking that every single person who sees you isn't wishing to take you home—then you're wrong. So terribly wrong."

"Then what do you say? How about you make me feel good for a little longer tonight?" I purr.

With a growl he grabs me by the hand, pulling me toward his SUV as he unlocks it and opens the back door for me. I climb up with him following close behind, and as soon as he slams the door, I pull him by his shirt to me.

We kiss again, feverishly, wild, and messy. His hands are in my hair, on my ass, on my neck as he continues to kiss my lips. Alex traces kisses all over my neck and to my ear before saying, "Here I thought elves were on the nice list."

"I'd rather be naughty all day," I whisper, unbuckling his belt and pulling his pants down until his dick springs free.

"You're going to kill me, woman," he groans.

"What a way to go," I add, grabbing my purse from the floor of the SUV and pulling out a condom. I roll it over his dick as he continues to kiss my neck and palm my breasts. He runs his hands all over my body until he makes his way under my dress, pulling my panties down and helping me take them off. The space is awkward as fuck between this giant taking up most of the room and my big ass bumping into everything, but neither of us complains. Our gasps and grunts reverberate through the cabin as we manage to keep our balance and get half-naked.

Once my underwear is off, Alex brings his calloused hands back up my thighs and squeezing my ass gently he groans,

"You have the most perfect ass. It's a shame it was hiding under all that fabric." He caresses my hip and the dip right above my pussy as he uses his thumb to slide between my lips and press gently on my clit.

"Oh God," I whisper at the contact. I know I'm wet; I don't need to feel his finger sliding in and out easily to know. I can feel my wetness sliding down between my thighs, but it is even hotter when his eyes light up with fire at his discovery.

"So wet, Liv, so hot," he whispers against my lips as he teases my clit with his thumb and my entrance with two fingers.

"Stop teasing and fuck me already," I beg, circling my hips against his hand. "Someone could walk by at any time, and then we'd be interrupted. What a shame that would be."

He picks me up by my hips and I use my hands as leverage. When I feel his dick at my entrance, I slide over it, feeling so full immediately. "Mmm," I purr.

"Fuck, you feel so good," he gaps with a low growl as he uses his hands to tilt my hips forward and back.

I dig my knees into the cold leather seat and bring my hips up, sliding up and down on him—faster and harder, pulling delicious sounds out of his throat. I begin riding him with everything I have and more. It feels so good, it won't be long before I burst into flames. I continue the movement, reveling in the guttural sounds Alex is emitting, and when he lifts his fingers to pinch my nipples over the fabric of my dress, I arch my back against him and pick up my tempo.

"That's it," he growls as he feels my pussy tightening around him. I squeeze my inner muscles tighter as I move up and down, my hands looping around his neck as I pull him closer to me. It takes two more rolls of my hips before I combust and I'm riding the high. I feel him tense and grunt at the same time I let out a moan, and he pushes into me one more time before shaking beneath me.

I slow my pace, stretching the wave of pleasure. Our skin

is slick with sweat as our breaths even out, coming down from the most exhilarating high I've had in a while.

"What a kiss," I whisper against his ear, my words earning me a chuckle.

"What a kiss indeed," Alex replies.

This is when shit always gets awkward, so to minimize it, I slide off of his dick as quickly as possible. Without saying a word, I grab my purse and try to climb out of the SUV.

"Wait," he says, grabbing my hand that is on the door handle.

I attempt to brush him off. "It's okay, Alex. I need to go before it's midnight and the spell breaks. This was fun, thank you."

"Can I at least get your number?" he asks, unsure of himself and searching my eyes for answers.

I shake my head. "Honestly? I think it's best if we just let it be this way. If we ever see each other again, though, I'll give you my number. Have a good night." I wink at him and lean forward to kiss him on his beard-covered cheek as I open the SUV door and step out.

He sits there with his dick still out and completely dumbfounded as I close the door and make my way into my car. As soon as I'm safely inside, I blast the AC on high. I was shivering before, but that whole exchange has left my skin hot. I drive home happily sated.

ELEVEN DAYS BEFORE CHRISTMAS

ON THE ELEVENTH day of Christmas, Baker Oaks gave to me a proposal we couldn't refuse…

5

———

AN ASSHOLE EVERYONE HATES
BUBBLY, COLBIE CAILLAT

LIVIE

"ARE you going to tell me about what happened last night, or am I going to have to beg for details?" Hailey, my best friend and roommate, asks as we walk with our arms looped around each other. We had decided to brave the Christmas market, which is currently bustling with life.

The air is crisp, a welcome relief from the usual heat of Florida. Twinkling lights dangle overhead between all the small businesses' stalls, weaving through their doors and windows. The scent of cinnamon and roasted nuts fills the air as Christmas carols play at almost every vendor's station.

Baker's Christmas Market is always fun. The day starts with a parade and the school band playing for the whole town. Sixth Street is closed to vehicles, allowing only foot traffic, making it a lot more manageable.

"Not much to tell, Hales. I went, he was a dick, so I left," I answer, walking fast and trying not to bump into anyone.

"Then why did it take you so long to get home if it was

33

such a bust?" Hailey questions, lifting her eyebrows and matching my pace.

I look up at her and bite my lips. I'm sure I'm blushing, too.

"Livie! What did you do? Did you fuck Frank from finance?" she asks, nudging my shoulder playfully.

"Shh! This is a family event." I force a laugh as I dodge a kid darting past, clutching a candy cane as big as his head. "And to answer your question, no, I didn't fuck Frank. The hot probably six-five-foot Adonis of a man, though? Him, I fucked thoroughly in the back of his SUV." I continue walking like I didn't just reveal my latest escapade to my best friend in the middle of a public market.

We pass a stall draped in red and green where a woman is selling handmade ornaments. I catch a glimpse of a sparkling glass star, and it reminds me of when I was little. All I wanted was to hang my own ornaments on the tree, but my mother would only allow the ones she deemed perfect to go on it. That little sparkling star would've been my choice, but it would've never passed her approval.

I look to my side and notice Hailey's not there anymore. I turn to find her and see she's frozen in place, her eyes wide and sparkling with curiosity.

I rush back to her and say, "Stop being dramatic! Like you haven't had sex in the back of a vehicle before."

"Yeah, but I never just nonchalantly told my best friend without any details whatsoever! Spill," she snaps as she links her arm with mine and we continue walking.

"Well, remember, first I had the date with Frank. That went as well as I expected; it didn't last long at all and I left pissed." We stop in front of a vendor selling hot cocoa and order a couple with whipped cream and a dash of sprinkles. The air is crisp, and for this Florida girl, that means I get to drink all the hot drinks and wear all my cute winter clothes without feeling like people will roll their eyes at me. I enjoy this weather more than anything and the hot cocoa will be icing on the cake.

"Mm-hm," Hailey hums as she grabs her hot cocoa and takes a sip.

"Well, after I left, I sat by the water to just listen to the waves, and I guess I fell asleep. The next thing I knew, I opened my eyes and this handsome—no, not handsome, more like hot as sin—man with dirty blonde hair and gorgeous blue eyes was sitting by me. He scared the shit out of me, but I guess he saw me sleeping alone and he was keeping an eye on me. I don't know…it was sweet and weird and hot. Is that even possible?"

"Sounds like a book, to be honest," Hailey smirks.

I take a long sip of the hot cocoa, tasting the rich choco-late mixed with a hint of cinnamon. The whipped cream is smooth against my tongue and I close my eyes, humming at the taste. "It was quite hot. Well, we chatted for a minute, I accused him of stalking me because he also said he saw me leave the date, and he was just a bit shocked about my outfit."

"Well duh, Livie. You had a costume on."

"I was going to a party," I defend.

"And nobody else knew that."

"What? I was just going to be walking around dressed like that for no reason?"

"With how confidently you hold yourself? Nobody would even question it. But what happened next?"

"Well, we bantered for a bit and then he asked me to have dinner with him and we went to Yummy's. He didn't even bat an eyelash at the amount of food I ordered, and honestly? That was hot, too. And there I was, on a Friday night, having dinner with Thor personified and then one thing led to another. It was *so hot*."

"You forgot to tell her about the parking spot you stole from me," a voice says from behind us. I jump and tense at the same time.

We both turn around quickly, and my eyes widen at the sight of Alex standing there, looking just as good as he did yesterday, but now with the biggest smirk I've ever seen.

"Hi!" I shout, not sounding crazy at all.

"Hello, Livie. I took great pleasure in hearing all about your experience last night, but somehow you forgot to tell your friend here…" he pauses, gesturing to Hailey to say her name.

"Hailey," she replies breathlessly.

I snort and bring my hot cocoa to my mouth, trying to hide my smile. She looks at me with a deadly stare, shooting daggers at me.

"…your friend, Hailey, about how you stole my parking spot and flipped me off before all that happened. Also, Livie, it's not good manners to kiss and tell, you know?" Alex adds and I want the earth to swallow me whole.

It's Hailey's turn to snort this time, and I can't help but smile and roll my eyes. What else am I supposed to do? I got busted big time. I take a deep breath in an attempt to gather my bearings and rest my hands on my hips as I say, "Well, Alex, I was just telling Hailey here how subpar last night was."

He grins at me, his eyes trained on mine. He scratches his beard and replies, "Your dinner with that guy? Sure. Your dinner with me? Anything but. But you can keep lying to yourself. It was nice seeing you again, Liv."

There it is, that nickname again. From someone I just met? I shouldn't love it as much as I do but I do, nonetheless. He turns his body around as if he's going to walk away from me.

"Wait!" I shout, and Alex stops dead in his tracks, turning around slowly to face me.

"Yes?" he asks, unable to hide his grin.

"Let's try this again, shall we?" I ask and he nods. "Hey, Alex!., Sorry I was airing our dirty laundry to my best friend, but last night was fun and it deserved to be relived."

"Now *that* sounds like the truth. And regardless, I was just giving you a hard time. Although I would suggest not talking about explicit content in public. You know, Santa's always watching," he teases.

I take a sip of my hot cocoa, the warmth spreading through me like a hug as I blink slowly and let the moment between us pass.

"Alright, well, now I'm definitely the third wheel. Can we move on, or do I need to go home and let you two strip each other naked with your eyes some more?" Hailey interrogates, and we both laugh.

"Sorry. Where are my manners?" I quip with an eye roll. "Alex, this is Hailey. Hailey this is—"

I get interrupted by Hailey saying, "Alex Haddock. So nice to officially meet you. My family and I are big fans."

Big fans? When I asked him yesterday if he was famous and he said *something like that,* I thought he was bullshitting me. Now, Hailey seems to not only know who he is, but also she's a big fan.

"Uh, really? I thought I lost all of those." His flashing smile disappears as he puts his hands in his pocket. Last night when we first talked, he looked a little grumpy, maybe even shy. But now he seems sad after that comment.

"Why? Because the media seem to think you're this asshole who hates everyone? That might be true, but your true fans are still out there. Especially people from your hometown," Hailey insists, smiling at him.

He stays silent, looking at her with puzzled eyes before nodding. His shoulders relax and he turns his face to look at me.

"So, Livie, Thor of a man?" Alex asks, raising his eyebrow at me and bringing his thumb to my upper lip, sliding it softly over it. That single touch raises goosebumps all over my skin. "Just a little whipped cream," he adds when he sees my confusion, and then he gently sucks his thumb into his mouth.

"Oh my God! Get a room," Hailey shouts. "I'm leaving; you two have fun!"

I shake my head. "No, Hails, wait. You and I were here together. Alex can go on his merry way."

"Nah, it's okay. You two," she says, looking at us both and laughing gently, "you two can continue this whole sexual tension situation without a spectator. Be safe children, be safe." She turns on her heels and walks back to where her car is parked.

"Is she always that blunt?" Alex asks.

"Yup," I say, popping the 'p' and nodding. "You should see her with people she knows—she's obnoxiously direct."

"You mean like you? Not obnoxious, obviously, but direct to the max."

"I am not," I protest, crossing my arms over my chest.

This pulls a smile from his face. "*I bet you have plenty of room in that big SUV of yours*," he says, mimicking my voice from last night. I'm sure now I'm blushing because suddenly, in the light of day, I don't feel as bold or forward as I was last night. I can feel the heat rising up my neck to my cheeks and when he chuckles, I know he can tell.

"It's okay, Livie. I like it," he adds.

"Okay. Are you going to tell me what that whole *I'm a fan* was about, though?" I ask.

"How about we go to lunch and I'll tell you? You did say you'd give me your number if I saw you again."

We stand there in silence, suspended in time, the world passing us by and disappearing from sight. If I read this scene in one of my romance books, I would roll my eyes and blame it on instant love, but I'm pretty sure this is insta-lust more than anything. Even if I wanted to say no, I couldn't, because my fingers are itching to touch his skin. My lips tingle with the thought of kissing him again, and my heart is thumping fast and hard at the possibility of spending more time with him.

I take a step forward and link my arm with his. "Lead the way."

6

HOLY SHIT, THAT'S HUGE
USE SOMEBODY, KINGS OF LEON

ALEX

WE WALK in silence to the end of Sixth and Magnolia. I open the glass door to Ronnie's, our local diner, and let Livie go in first. When I told Nick I was going to the Market to see Nat and Bella, I didn't think I was going to run into Livie. What are the odds that I would see my hook up from last night in my hometown? Last night was both a blur and a dream. I sound like a poet even thinking about it, but the connection I shared with her was nothing I've experienced before. Hooking up with women is not new to me, but there was something different about her that screamed *more*—but then one thing led to another, and I followed what I wanted. I shouldn't have, but I did.

"Welcome to Ronnie's! Anything to drink?" the waitress asks. I eat at Ronnie's a lot, but I usually choose to pick up rather than dining in, so I haven't learned all the employee's names. But there's something oddly familiar about this waitress.

"Hey, Nells," Livie greets. "Can I get the usual starter please?"

"Livie! I haven't seen you since forever. Sorry, I didn't notice it was you and yes, yes you can. What about you, Alex?" the waitress asks and now I feel like a douche for not remembering her name.

"Water for me, thanks."

"You got it." She walks to the back of the restaurant, disappearing through wooden doors.

"So, Alex," Livie starts both elbows on top of the table, linking her fingers together under her chin. "Do you live in Baker? First Hailey, and now Nellie know you by name. And that's odd, considering I've never seen you before."

Nellie. Of course, she looked familiar—her sister Cara is one of my closest friends. I forgot her little sister is not so little anymore.

I clear my throat. "Born and raised, but I could say the same thing about you."

"Not born and raised, but I moved here a few years ago. I grew up in Magnolia Springs, just an hour south of here, but Hailey loves Baker Oaks. So after college, we moved here. I love it and never want to leave."

I wish I could say the sentiment was mutual, and the truth is I used to love living in Baker, but tainted memories have made it very difficult to have a life here. A slow-paced life. A comfortable life. My house is what some people dream about, and I like it, but it's missing something. Mom thinks it's missing holiday cheer and grandchildren, and maybe she's right. I'm afraid I might never give her what she wants since I'm almost thirty and have not had a steady relationship with pretty much anyone.

"Back to you being famous, though. Am I going to have to Google you? Holy shit, if I Google you, am I going to find a bunch of dirt on you?" Livie asks and I flinch. A bunch of dirt on me is exactly what she will find on the Internet and I don't want her to see any of that. I want her to see who I am now. Who I've always been, when I'm not trying to recover from a life-changing injury.

"You can, but I can just tell you. I used to play football, and you know people in the South and their football. They make it a bigger deal than it is, I promise." I grab my water from Nellie's hand as she stands right next to us, welcoming the distraction. She places a plate in front of Livie with fried green tomatoes and ranch.

"How big are we talking, though? High school, college ball? Ah, thank you, Nells. You're an angel."

"More like he was the QB for the Rhinos," Nellie adds and Livie's eyes go wide.

"Holy shit, that's huge! Well, congrats on retirement," she spits out before turning back to Nellie and ordering her entree. I order mine quickly and then stay quiet, hoping she doesn't make a big deal of this and waiting for the conversation to continue. When it doesn't, I look up and find Livie watching me with tenderness in her eyes.

"Did I say something wrong?" Livie asks, her dark wavy hair cascading over one shoulder as she studies me.

"No, why?" I reply, trying to shake off the heaviness that has settled in.

"You got really quiet, and I can't pinpoint when or why. Was it because I didn't know who you were? I'm sorry, Alex, I don't watch much TV. And my family follows baseball, not football, so I don't hear much about it."

"It really is nothing to worry about," I answer, the lie sliding off my lips like a knife over butter—smooth but sharp. It's not a complete lie, just a partial one. I don't talk much about football, but everyone around me does. *When are you going to talk about your injury? Are you going back to football, even if you don't play? What happened at that party? Did you really kill a man over a photograph? Is it true that the American Football Association paid you to quit the team?*

Rumors, lies, bullshit—that's what I don't want, so I mostly stay out of conversations about it. Football is dead to me; but as much as I want everyone to forget I ever played, it doesn't look like it's happening any time soon. I can't even get volunteer opportunities because people are afraid that I'm volatile or a liability. I don't blame them, but I need to figure out who I am now without it.

"Then we don't have to talk about football at all," she says, shrugging her shoulder as she takes a bite of the fried green tomato on her plate. It's a simple gesture, but I can tell she means it.

"Thanks," I reply, trying to muster a smile. "I appreciate that. It's just…a lot."

Livie nods, her gaze softening. "We all have our baggage. What do you want to talk about instead?" She leans in with her soft smile and her pretty brown eyes.

I pause, contemplating my response while I sip my drink. "I guess I'm still figuring that out. But I'd like to know more about you. What's your story?"

Her eyes light up in amusement as she raises an eyebrow and answers, "Well, I guess a change of topic *is* what you wanted. Okay, I'll bite. You already know I live here and that I grew up in Florida. You know my best friend is Hailey and you know my taste in men is outstandingly different from my mother's, considering she hasn't been able to set me up with a proper date in forever…but it still led me to a man watching me sleep. Then you end up being the best company I've had in a while. Is that sad?"

I lean in snickering and add, "Sad for her, for sure, but for us, it sounds like it was meant to be. I happen to enjoy your company too, and I don't enjoy many people. What do you do for a living?"

"I work at the children's hospital, offering support to children in hospice or in long-term hospital care. Nothing teaches you to appreciate life, and what you have, more than seeing how fragile it can be." Livie smiles softly, and I can't help but smile back.

"Sounds like you're a good person," I say, feeling both sad and happy, I guess. I can tell by the tone of her voice she loves it and she makes a difference, but it's probably so damn hard doing that as a job.

"Oh no, no, don't do that! Don't look at me with those puppy eyes, like I'm broken or a masochist. It's hard, yes, but I truly enjoy being there in the hardest part of their lives. I don't want a dark cloud looming over us, though. What do you do now that you don't play the sport everyone loves?"

"I'm still trying to figure it out." My voice trails off as I look down at my plate, and I push around the food with my fork. The truth is, this topic causes more turmoil inside of me than I'd like to admit.

"Aren't we all?" she replies, her tone light but her eyes searching mine for something more.

Just then Nellie arrives, balancing our entrees on a tray with ease. She sets down our plates, the aroma wafting up like a warm embrace. "Enjoy, you guys! Holler if you need anything." She beams at us, her energy is infectious, but I can't help but feel a shadow hovering over my thoughts.

As I take a bite, I steal a glance at Livie. She seems at ease, her features softening as she eats her food. "What are you trying to figure out, Livie? You seem pretty content." The words come out easily. She's easy to talk to, funny, and beautiful as hell too.

"I am. Content, that is. I'm actually happy. I love my life. I enjoy my job and I have a solid friendship with Hailey. My mother doesn't seem to think being content or even happy is enough if I'm still single, and I'm a little tired of it." Her voice has a slight edge, revealing the frustration beneath her bubbly personality. It's funny to see her share so much with me, a near-perfect stranger. She's so open, but her mom—who is supposed to know her—doesn't see she's not helping.

"What are you going to do about it?" I ask, trying to sound nonchalant, but I can feel the urgency creeping into my voice. I know damn well I need to do something about my own problems, and the thought hangs heavy in the air between us.

She shrugs, her smile faltering for just a moment. "Short of showing up with a boyfriend to Christmas Eve dinner, I don't think there's much I can do." She takes a bite of her food and tilts her head to the side, looking at what she just ate. She frowns as if it tastes bad.

"What?" I ask, wondering if there's something wrong with her meal.

She lets out a soft laugh and shakes her head. "Have you ever taken a bite of something while looking at something else, and your brain can't comprehend what just happened? Well, I was looking at your food while I took a bite of this, and I thought I was short-circuiting." We both laugh now.

Her words keep playing in my head over and over again, even though she has changed the topic to something else. *Short of showing up with a boyfriend to Christmas Eve dinner, I don't think there's much I can do.*

"Can I ask why your mother is so focused on you dating someone?"

"Old-fashioned tradition of her homeland and me being almost thirty. It's bullshit, to be honest. Don't get me wrong—I'm not running away from a potential relationship. I would love nothing more than to date someone and maybe see if marriage and settling down is in the future. But it has to be someone worthy of my time and my heart. I have worked too hard to be where I am now, physically, mentally, and emotionally, to fuck it up with people like Frank from finance."

I snort at that, which earns me another pretty smile from her. Livie's smile is wide and bright with deep dimples in her cheeks. She has perfect teeth and they compliment her expression perfectly. She's anatomically beautiful all the way to even the shade on the enamel of her teeth. She's so pretty it hurts. It hurts to be sitting across from her and not drag her over the table and kiss her senseless again.

"I'm turning thirty next year and I feel like if I show up by myself to this stupid dinner, I will never hear the end of it. But I don't want to string people along or give the wrong impression, so I might skip this year's dinner."

"Have you ever skipped one before?"

"Nope, not in my almost thirty years of life."

Her words resonate with me more than I expected. I've been wrestling with so much uncertainty in my own life. But what sticks with me is that she's willing to skip something that's meaningful to her to avoid confrontation or being uncomfortable. My image—how I present myself to the world, how others perceive me—is not who I am. And after letting the media run wild with allegations, I have buried myself in disgrace. She doesn't want to disappoint her mom. I want to stop disappointing mine.

"What if I come with you?" I ask, letting the words slip out before I can stop them.

Livie coughs, covering her mouth to keep from spitting out whatever it is she's eating. "To where? To my mother's house?"

"Yeah. What if you bring me and we can pretend we're together for her sake?"

"Alex, I don't even know your full name."

"Alexander James Haddock."

"Not what I meant."

"That's what you said."

"Are you always this literal? You can't mean it. My mom is part psychic; she would know immediately something was up and what? I'm just going to show up with you and hope for the best when I don't even know your favorite color?"

I open my mouth to answer but she lifts her finger in warning as she raises her eyebrow.

"Also, not what I meant. I barely know you," she adds.

I shrug, trying not to smirk. "We can change that."

"So…what? I rocked your world last night and now all of a sudden you want to go out with me so I can show my mother I'm dateable?" Livie scoffs. "That sounds ridiculous."

"Well, not entirely that," I reply, grabbing my cup and taking a sip. Getting Livie to help me could be a game-changer. She's got that effortless charm, a knack for turning heads. If I could tap into that, maybe I could reshape how people see me. If I could be seen with this ball of Christmas spirit, maybe people would finally let me be who I truly am and not who they want me to be.

"What if I have a way for you to help me, too?" I thought she would be game, but her expressionless face is making me second-guess myself. As I look at her, I wonder if she'd want to be part of any of it. Would she see my mess as a burden? Does she think I'm only talking to her so she can help me? The thoughts make my heart race, but there's a flicker of hope. Maybe, just maybe, if I open up, we could tackle our issues together. "I could use a little help on showing people I'm not who they think I am."

Her expression shifts to curiosity as she folds both hands under her chin in her *I'm listening* pose, which I've noticed in the two short days I've known her. "What do you mean?"

I take a deep breath, stirring my drink with a straw and mirroring Livie's sudden movements. "I've been trying to figure out who I am now that football is…well, done. But no matter how hard I try, people don't seem to let it go. The rumors are exhausting, and I feel like I need a fresh start. But no one seems to see me beyond the party boy. All they see is Alex the troublemaker."

Livie nods, her expression thoughtful. "I get that. People can be quick to judge based on what they hear or what they think they know."

"You have no idea," I reply.

"Then enlighten me, Alex. I don't work today and now that Hailey left, my agenda just cleared up."

"I played for the NFL, right? All good, except I was a little reactive. I partied too much. I got into a couple of fights. I was caught screaming at the paparazzi more times than I can count. I got injured, which is why I don't play anymore; the recovery was brutal for both my physical and mental health. I said things I shouldn't have and I caused a scene in a few public places. Bar fights, screaming at paparazzi, leaving places drunk—I was a mess and I'm not proud of it."

"Okay, but you clearly are not an asshole. So what changed?" she asks.

"Promise not to laugh?"

"I can't promise but I'll try," she answers, softening her features.

"I went to therapy and learned how to cope with a lot of shit. I do yoga once a week and I go on daily walks at the farm."

She smiles at me, and this time her whole body seems like it's melting as she grabs my hand and says, "So you are a public grump who is really a closeted hippie?" I nod and she continues, "There's nothing to be ashamed of, about any of that. I'm glad you found what helps. It takes courage to try new things. I can't imagine how much people judged you when you showed up to yoga with all those giant muscles."

I let out a soft laugh and reply, "Not too harsh, but I still haven't had any luck showing people I'm not that angry kid anymore. And I think you could help me. If you're willing, of course."

Livie tilts her head, intrigued. "How?"

I hesitate, then say, "What if we pretended to date? It could work in both our favor. I'd help you get your mom off your back about settling down, and I'd get a chance to redefine how people see me."

She raises an eyebrow, a mix of surprise and amusement

dancing in her eyes. "Fake dating? Also, what do I have that would help people see you differently?"

"The media is used to seeing me with different girls—not my finest moment—and nobody like you."

"What? Chunky and short like a cupcake?" she whisper-shouts.

I'm wide-eyed as I shake my head at whatever bullshit she thinks I meant. "You're not chunky, Livie. You're beautiful."

"Oh my God, please don't be this person. I said chunky, not ugly, and I am. I don't have a problem with it—do you?"

How the fuck did this conversation turn into this? "Wait, wait. I don't think you understood me, and I'm so sorry if I said something wrong. I just… fuck. Sorry. What I meant by girls like you is sweet, kind, bubbly girls. You were actually dressed like an elf on a random Friday. You work with sick children. And your smile… Well, your smile can light up a whole room, Liv. It had nothing to do with your body. I fucking love your body."

She lets out a breath and says, "Okay. That makes sense, I guess… sorry I snapped. I've also worked hard at loving every inch of me, but I'm used to people who just see me as the fat sweet girl, but not the whole me, you know?"

"It's okay. Sorry, it took a turn."

We stay silent, waiting for some words to magically appear.

"Did calling myself chunky make you uncomfortable?" Livie offers. "I'm ripping the band-aid off now."

What do I say? Yes, it did, and risk her thinking I'm superficial? Or do I lie? "Honestly, Livie, I'm not sure. I think so, but I think it's because I feel like girls hate that word and I've only heard it in negative ways. I don't know. Sorry."

"Stop apologizing, please. It's okay to not know. But just so we're clear, I love my body the way it is and I didn't mean it in a bad way. I'm chunky, curvy, fat, plus size—it's fine. It's part of who I am, not *all* that I am."

"I like your body, in case it wasn't obvious last night," I reply, smiling softly at her and reaching for her hand across the table. "But I also like you, all of you. I know it sounds crazy because we just met, but I had such a good time last night. It doesn't happen often."

"Thanks, boo. Now tell me more about your plan. Do you really think it could work?"

"Why not?" I chuckle. "We could pull it off. Just think of it as a fun little project. I mean I would date the hell out of you but starting to date someone just so we can get something out of it, doesn't seem fair. Pretend to date and have fun while at it sounds better, don't you think?"

Livie takes a moment to consider, then smirks. "Okay, but only if you promise to be charming and not a total disaster. Also, no more freaking out over words—we're both adults and we can talk."

"I can do charming," I reply, the corners of my mouth lifting. "I can do honest, too, and I can also talk. Just don't expect me to wear matching outfits or anything."

"Deal," she laughs, shaking her head. "But I can't promise my mom won't start planning the wedding as soon as she sees us so you better get ready."

"Guess I better brace myself," I say, feeling a genuine connection between us. Now all that is left is figuring out what to do next.

NINE DAYS BEFORE CHRISTMAS

ON THE NINTH day of Christmas Baker Oaks gave to me reading to children and a viral post.

7

———

SHORTIE

KID ON CHRISTMAS, PENTATONIX
FT. MEGHAN TRAINOR

LIVIE

Me: Do you have plans today?

Alex: Hello to you too.

Alex: No, I don't.

Me: Want to come read to children?

Alex: No, not really.

Me: It'll be fun.

Alex: Would it make me an asshole if I say I don't like kids?

Me: Yes

Me: I mean, no it won't make you an asshole. It would just make me really sad

Me: Like really, really sad

Me: So sad

Alex: Fine, I like them but they don't like me

Me: My kids will love you. Just come to the hospital this afternoon. It'll be good and we can talk more about your crazy plan

Alex: You already said yes

Me: Yeah well, we have 9 days before Christmas which means there are 8 days before the dinner for me to learn everything about you so my mother doesn't suspect anything and 8 days for me to convince the world you're not an asshole

Alex: Maybe I am

Me: FML

Me: You're not obvs

Me: I'm here until 6:00. Come read to the children and I might even let you take me to dinner

Alex: Are you asking me out, Liv?

Me: No, I'm telling you you're taking me out.

Alex: Fine, what should I bring?

Me: Yourself, an open mind and a smile. I have a book here.

Alex: See you in an hour

Me: Deal

"WHY ARE you bouncing around more than normal, Livie?" Cassie, the head nurse asks. With her short blonde bob, her pretty blue eyes and the soft smile she wears 90% of the time, Cassie is the definition of a hug in human form. The best friend everyone wished they had, and the mom so many kids wished they could call hers. But we all just call her Nurse Cass around here. She's everyone's favorite nurse and one of my closest friends.

"You're just jealous I'm always in a good mood and you're not."

"I'm always in a good mood," she replies, adding some papers to her clipboard and placing it under her desk.

"No, you always *look* like you're in a good mood when in reality, you just hide all your anger behind the hospital mom look you're sporting."

"I can let my anger out on stupid diseases taking the lives of children, not on humans I love. All that anger you see behind my eyes? Are for things I cannot change. However, the usual tornado you live in is a lot wilder today. You've been singing and swirling as you go. More than usual that is. You even smiled at Miles."

Miles is the jerk resident on rounds tonight. He acts like he's all that and a bag of chips when he's not and we fucking hate him. But nothing can sour my mood today. I'm seriously considering telling her all about Alex and our deal, but we promised to keep it between us. Am I really this giddy about seeing him again? I saw him yesterday and the day before—hell, I just met the guy. But he's a funny, almost grumpy gentleman who looks like Thor and talks like he has more than half a neuron. I'm positive my body doesn't know what to do with those feelings.

"Hello! Earth to Livie," Cassie calls, waving her hand in front of me, pulling me back to reality.

"Okay, okay, do you really want to know?" I ask, laying myself across her desk and smiling at her like an idiot.

"Yes. Dear lord, child, please tell me you didn't sleep with Fred."

"Frank," I say in between a snort and a laugh. "Nah, the only reason I told you I was going out with him was just so that, in case you didn't hear from me, you could come to my rescue and kill him."

"Then what is it?!" she shouts. But before I can answer, there's a deep voice coughing near us. We both look and there, standing dressed in dark denim jeans and a navy-blue Henley that makes his eyes look lighter, is Alex. He has his hand in his pocket, the other holding a coffee, and a shy smile on his lips that also suits him just fine.

"How can I help you?" Cassie asks, smiling at him and going into Nurse Cassie mode. Zero games—just pure work.

"I'm here to see the kids and umm… Livie." He points at me and Cassie's head snaps my way.

"I got it, Cass." I look up and smile at Alex, forgetting how tall he is until I'm standing right in front of him and he needs to make a conscious effort looking down to meet my eyes. I tuck a strand of my wavy hair behind my ear. "Hey, Alex."

"Hey shortie," he whispers, only for me to hear, with his mischievous smile and his wintery scent. He smells like a bakery on a cold Christmas day—sweet, warm, and spicy.

"shortie?" I ask, raising an eyebrow.

"Testing it out. See if it fits. It does, doesn't it?"

"Maybe…but don't call me that in front of the kids."

"What should I call you?"

"Ms. Livie. Come on, let's get you checked in."

My hospital ID badge feels cold against my skin as I pull it up and down, fidgeting with it while walking Alex a few feet down to the registration desk. "So, this is it," I explain, my voice a little higher than usual. The children's wing lobby buzzes with a low hum—the soft cries of babies, hushed parental whispers, and the squeak of a gurney disappearing around a corner. The open floor plan of this hospital makes it really easy to find things but really hard to find calm, peace, and quiet.

He grunts, his gaze glued to the floor. "Peachy," he mumbles, looking around and fidgeting with his hands.

I sigh. "Look, it's just kids. It will be fine. They will love you and—" I say, getting closer and looking up at him "—I have a plan."

We approach the volunteer desk and tell Rosalie, the registrar, that Alex is here to volunteer today. "Welcome, Alex! Have you filled out the paperwork online?" she asks with a bright smile.

He shakes his head. "I… uh… no not really." He looks sheepish for a split second. Nothing like the confident man I've met these past three days.

Rosalie chuckles. "No worries, it happens. We have copies here. Just need your name, address, and emergency contact…" She explains the process, and I watch as Alex, despite his initial reluctance, begins to engage with her. By the time the paperwork is done, their conversation is over as well, and Rosalie is flushed and laughing so loud. It seems like she's working overtime.

She's flipping her hair and batting her eyelashes at him, on top of giggling like a schoolgirl. I don't blame her; she's young and he is… well, hot as sin, and nice. I narrow my eyes at her and when she notices, she coughs slightly and goes back to her paperwork.

"Come on, Alex, let's go see the children."

He waves goodbye to her, walking side by side with me until we make it to the double doors with the key fob ready for me to scan my badge.

"Ms. Livie!" I hear some of the children shout loudly as soon as they see me. Lisa is jumping on her rolling bed, waving frantically and holding zero back as usual, and Laurie already has a pile of books on the table next to her. I told her earlier today I was going to bring a friend by and to meet me in the children's area with some books. She's also a child, but if I were to remind her that, she would come for my head. Laurie is twelve and is currently here in rehab after a transplant. She hates everything and everyone in a true twelve-year-old fashion, but not me. She adores me and I'm running with it.

"Hello, my little sugarplums! Who's ready for some stories?" I ask, making a drumroll on my lap and they all join in. I started storytime a few years ago when one of the little ones here for long-term care was sad her parents couldn't read to her as energetically as her teacher had. Even though she was in a hospital homebound school, she still wanted an in-person read-aloud. I started reading to her, sometimes dressing up and sometimes just showing up—and the word spread. Soon, I had a bunch of kids parked outside of her room waiting for me each day, so we moved it to the media center, and the rest was history. I won't give up my Sunday shifts for anything.

"Today, I have a special guest for you. This is my friend Alex and he's here to read you a wonderful story. He's a little nervous, so make sure you make him feel welcome," I say.

"Ms. Livie?" Lisa asks with her beautiful bold head and her bright blue eyes.

"Yes, sweetie?"

"Is he a BFG?" she asks and I look at her with a puzzled look. "You know," she insists, "the Big Friendly Giant?"

I can't stop the laughter that bubbles from deep within me and reverberates through my bones. I look up at Alex—who is currently red as tomato– but he's laughing too. His shoulders are relaxing and his eyes softening.

I plan on intervening and saying something nice to divert attention, but Alex beats me to it and says, "I'm not a giant but I'm friendly enough. Ms. Livie tells me you guys love stories. Now I can't promise I'll be as entertaining as her but I can try. Where should I sit?"

The kids all laugh and smile at him. *He's a natural,* I think to myself as I point to where I usually sit to read and he takes the spot. He looks ridiculous. Good, but ridiculous; with his broad shoulders, his long legs spilling from the bench like spider legs, and how giant he looks next to the rest of the children gathered around him. I suppress a laugh because what else can I do?

He looks around until he finds me and smiles softly at me, shrugging. I smile back and point at the pile of books Laurie gathered. They're all Christmas books and I can't wait to see which one he picks.

He opens one of my favorites and, after taking a deep breath in and shutting his eyes for a split second, he starts reading. His voice is shaky at first but as he continues reading, he starts changing his cadence with the story and characters. He grows more confident with each page. The children are enthralled and the room is completely quiet, other than by the echo of his voice. I grab my phone and snap a picture, tagging him—I found him online last night after our whole 'Christmas deal' conversation— and the hospital on social media with the caption *Tackling tales and scoring smiles.* I slide my phone into the pocket of my hot pink scrubs and sit on the ground next to Laurie.

"Your friend, huh?" she asks, wiggling her eyebrows at me.

I roll my eyes dramatically. "Oh hush, child, yes. He's my friend. Now listen to the story."

"It's for babies," she whispers.

"I don't know what you're talking about, I love this one."

"You're just a big baby Ms. Livie." She smiles at me but then stops talking, turning her face to Alex and listening to the story.

8

DO YOU TRUST ME?

I DON'T KNOW ABOUT YOU, CHRIS LANE

ALEX

"ALRIGHT, alright, no more. I draw the line at ten books," I say to the group of kids pouting in front of me. I lift my hands and look up, trying to find support in Livie, but instead she's smiling knowingly at me.

"But Mr. Alex, how can you say no to sick children?" The little brunette darling with pigtails in front of me pleads.

I'm sure my face shows the horror and shock before she laughs and shakes her head. "I'm just kidding. You can breathe now. If I can't make fun of this situation, who can?" she asks and I laugh. I've laughed more today than I have many years and it feels good.

"My little sugarplums, it's time to go back to what you were doing, and I'm sure I'll see you around in a bit." Livie chimes. I don't know how I managed to read so many stories without getting distracted every few minutes by her. She's wearing scrubs with ice cream print all over them and her hair is in two loose braids that frame her beautiful face. She looks different than the other night. I think the main difference—

other than the fact she isn't annoyed—is that she doesn't have makeup on. I like it a lot.

Livie walks out of the room, swaying her gorgeous hips with a slight bounce in her step. After she goes through the doors, with me following right behind her, she turns around and says, "You're a natural, Alex. That was incredible! And my plan worked—look." She shows me her phone, and I find she's pulled up a post of me reading one of the Christmas books the teenager with the death stare picked. It has… holy shit, thousands of likes and comments. I grab the phone from her and read through the comments. They're mostly people saying how amazing the picture is, some people asking how she got me to volunteer at the hospital, and some say, "Welcome back, Alex!"

When the whole press disaster happened, I decided to step away from socials because, in my case, no press was better than bad press, and I just never went back. I don't pay attention to this type of thing. But when I started reaching out to different organizations to see if they would let me host events or shadow some of theirs, I got zero open doors, and most of them were locked tight. I hope that by showing a different side of me—a softer side—maybe I will get opportunities to show others that I'm more than my mistakes. Isn't that what this holiday season is about either way? Forgiveness and celebration of the gifts we bring?

"Thank you," I say, handing her back her phone.

"Step one of Operation Make People Fall in Love with Alex done," Livie exclaims, punching both fists in the air in victory.

"You're a little genius, aren't you?" I ask, brushing a flyaway from her braid back from her face.

"Sometimes I am. I have to get back to work, though. Thank you so much for coming. Text you later?" she asks with a soft smile.

"I thought you were going to let me take you to dinner tonight."

"So, you're still on for that? If so, can I text you when I get home?"

"Please do," I reply. "Where do you want to go?"

"Somewhere in Baker?" she suggests, smiling at me.

"You got it. I'll see you tonight," I promise, grabbing her hand and bringing it to my mouth to kiss it softly.

"Bye, Alex," she whispers, waving softly.

"Bye, shortie."

I walk in silence to my SUV. Getting in and turning on the ignition, I smile to myself because I enjoyed that more than I thought I would. Although there was some surprise PR involved, it felt good just to do it. It felt wonderful to do something nice without expecting anything in return.

I PICKED Livie up after work and we went to Saddlers, our local country bar. Some of my high school friends were there and we hung out with them. Livie and the girls of the group hit it right off, and nothing made me happier. I got home, took a shower, and hopped into bed, ready for good sleep. This weekend was unexpected, but a good kind of unexpected.

Before I can close my eyes, I notice a glow from my nightstand. I don't keep my ringer on, so the only way for me to see a message is when the notification lights up the room. I hate the ringer and the sounds. Always have, always will. I grab my phone and see a text from Livie. I'm smiling like a stupid high schooler obsessing over his first crush.

Livie: Officially went viral

Me: Nah, just a lot of attention

Livie: No, no. I'm talking 1 million views.

Me: It'll be fine. People are just probably surprised there was a picture of me out and about. I've been hiding for a while.

Livie: With that pretty face? How?

Me: Liv, have you ever seen me before? And we live in the same town?

Livie: Touché, touché

Time passes by without another message from her. I find myself waiting with the phone in my hand to see if she'll say something else. I want to know more about her. I want to talk more. Right when I think she's done, I get another notification.

Livie: We have momentum going, I think we need to use it.

Me: We do. We do.

Livie: Do you trust me?

Even though I just met her, all I want to say is yes. Is it crazy? Maybe but I haven't had a good time with someone in a while and something tells me she truly means well.

Me: As crazy as it sounds, I think I do.

Livie: Pick me up tomorrow at 7:00pm. Wear something comfy and warm.

Me: Done

SEVEN DAYS BEFORE CHRISTMAS

On the seventh day of Christmas Baker Oaks gave to me a picnic at the park and a hot kiss by the SUV.

9

CAN I KISS YOU?
THIS TOWN, NIALL HORAN

ALEX

I'M WAITING on the wrap-around front porch of Livie's old Southern-style house with white siding and a deep green door. The temperature tonight is perfect, so even though I've been waiting for a few minutes, it's not uncomfortable. Whatever we decide to do tonight, I hope it's outside.

Last night I picked her up after work and we served hot cocoa at the park at a Christmas caroling event. We served it to all the kids and adults singing, as well as the patrons who went by. It was a lovely night and I had a lot of fun. She's so damn funny; I found myself laughing more than I have in years.

This morning, the Baker Gazette had a picture of us smiling on the front page with the heading "Grumpy and Sunshine: Are Alex Haddock's party days over?" And there was a whole article about Livie and me; the details speculating how this might be exactly what I need to straighten out my life. I'm sure hanging out with Livie and showing up to public events with her has helped, but I don't want her life to be completely disrupted by the media, so I'm trying to balance out the overly public outings.

When Livie opens the door, soft light illuminates everything about her and her beautiful eyes. Her hair cascades in loose waves, catching the light perfectly, and her smile is infectious. She's wearing jeans and an olive sweatshirt—that color was made just for her. She looks effortlessly beautiful and my breath catches.

"Hey, ready to go?" I ask, trying to keep my voice steady before I can give myself away. Five days. I've known this girl for five days and my heart already races.

"Absolutely!" she replies, her eyes sparkling with excitement. I don't even notice the basket she has until she passes by. I take it from her and after a cordial exchange of smiles, we head to the SUV and I open the door for her. As I slide into the driver's seat, I can't help but steal glances at her as she guides me to wherever it is we're going. The way she talks about little things with such enthusiasm draws me in deeper.

As we pull into the gravel lot beside the football field, I see the giant sign announcing an outdoor movie night. I haven't stepped foot on this field in forever, and my hands tighten around the steering wheel while my jaw snaps shut.

"Hey," Livie whispers, placing her hand over mine. "I'm sorry, I didn't think about the location when I was planning this. We can just leave."

I know it's just a place, but it brings so many memories and I just wasn't ready.

"It's okay. I'll be fine. It just took me by surprise." I find an empty spot near the entrance and step out of the SUV before she can say anything else. The atmosphere is festive, with people milling about carrying blankets and snacks. I can already hear the faint sound of Christmas music playing in the background.

I grab the basket she packed from the SUV bed and open

her door, helping her step out. "Are you sure?" Livie asks with a question in her eyes.

"I'm sure. I do have a question for you, though."

"What is it?"

"I've been thinking about this and yes, we've spent time together, we've posted about it and stuff but we're supposed to be dating, yeah?" I ask.

She raises an eyebrow. "Yes, I thought that's what we said."

"Okay, do we need to draw boundaries? You know, like physical affection and stuff." I search her eyes for regret or discomfort, but what I find is a smile. "I know we've spent a few days together already, but I just want to make sure."

"Are you trying to have your way with me on this football field, Alex?" She wiggles her brows and finds a cozy spot on the grass for the blanket. After spreading it out, I sit and lean back, taking in the view. I can't help but shake my head and smile.

"I just want to know what crosses the line. Can I hold your hand while we walk? Can I kiss you? Can I touch you? These past few days we've been pretty busy together, but this outing is completely public so I just want to make sure."

"You can do whatever you want. If I'm uncomfortable, I'll let you know. Does that sound like a plan?" she asks, opening the basket and getting two sodas out.

"Deal," I reply, grabbing her hand and pulling her to me. I kiss her forehead and keep her tucked against me. She gets her phone out and snaps a picture of us. My mouth is on the top of her head and her eyes are closed, smiling softly. If I didn't know better, I'd think we looked like a real couple. She invites me as a collaborator on her IG post, whatever that means, and with her help, I approve it so it shows in my account, too. I put my phone away and try to be in the moment. Her hair is soft under my chin. She smells like strawberries and something sweet. Like a dessert you can't get enough of. I must be pretty damn lonely if I'm so enthralled by someone I just met, but there's something about her.

The movie plays as we talk. We see some staring our way but other than that, nobody has bothered us and I'm thankful for it. I glance over at her. Her expression is focused, and I can't help but sneak a few looks at her profile. "So, any plans for the next few days?" I ask, trying to keep the conversation flowing. She turns to me, a smile lighting up her face, and we dive into a discussion about all the holiday events happening around town.

"There's a toy drive this weekend, and we could volunteer to wrap gifts at the bank," Livie suggests enthusiastically. I can't believe she's this involved in everything. She's constantly trying to make the best for everyone else. She offered to help with my public image, and she's making her mom happy by pretending to date me. But I realize I haven't even asked her about that.

"Has your mom said anything?"

Livie shakes her head. "She hasn't. But knowing her, she's waiting for me to say something. I wouldn't sweat it."

"Let me know if there's anything I can do to make her believe we're real, okay?"

"Yup. I'll tell her I'm bringing a plus one to dinner. I'm sure that'll get her talking."

After I bring up her mom, we lapse into a comfortable silence, letting the movie play in the background as I wonder if she's worried about how this will pan out in the end. We're both focused on the movie until she mentions something about her favorite Christmas food; just like that we fall into comfortable conversation. I realize how much I enjoy talking to her. It's easy and effortless, and I find myself wanting to be around her as much as possible. It sounds crazy but she makes everything feel brighter.

10

———

TWO FOR TWO
FEELS LIKE, GRACIE ABRAMS

LIVIE

THE MOVIE ENDED A WHILE AGO, but apparently, I fell asleep. A lot of my friends say I have an issue with falling asleep everywhere I go. I can sleep anywhere. But to be honest I think it's only an *issue* when it happens and I'm alone—like the other day on the bench. It happens so quickly I can't always prepare. I just need to lay my head somewhere comfortable, close my eyes, and sleep takes over—every time. If you add a comfortable, good-smelling man, well then, I guess I fall asleep faster.

Alex puts the basket in the back of his SUV as I lean against the side and smile at him.

"What?" he asks, returning my smile.

"Has anyone ever told you that you make a great pillow?" I tease.

"Nah, I don't actually think I've ever let anyone sleep on me before," he replies, tucking a piece of hair behind my ear. *Nobody?*

"Then why me?" I ask, incredulous.

71

"I told you, there are many reasons. One, I like you, Liv. I do. Two… I don't know, I'm comfortable around you and I don't feel like I have to put on a show. Three, you smell like strawberries and it's so damn good I want to bathe in it."

I'm sure I'm blushing if the heat rising up my cheeks is any indicator. I'm at a loss for words for once. He's looking at me with those intense hazel eyes filled with sincerity and his perfect damn face. I'm melting. A puddle under his gaze. "It's my soap," is the only stupid thing I can think to say. Sometimes, this line between whether this is fake dating or real dating is really blurry, especially in situations just like this one.

Alex chuckles a deep chuckle that I feel all the way down to my toes. "What's your soap?"

"The strawberry scent comes from my soap. A small shop downtown sells it. I'll get you some."

He smiles and steps closer to me, bringing his hand to my chin and softly tilting it up to him. His mouth hovers over mine. I close my eyes and catch my breath right before he says, "I don't need it as long as I'm close to you." His lips close over mine, kissing me gently at first.

His hips lock me in place, my back against his SUV and I suddenly can feel all of him. The hardness of his chest, his strong solid hands in contrast with his soft lips kissing me more intensely now. They are warm and soft against my own, and I part them softly to allow Alex to slide his tongue in. This kiss I feel in every inch of my body. His grip on my lower back tightens as I arch against him, and a soft moan escapes. The sound brings me back to reality and I remember where we are. I press my hands into his chest.

Alex responds immediately and stops. I can't believe I had to end this life-altering kiss. That's two for two, so the first one definitely wasn't a fluke.

"What a kiss," he whispers against my swollen lips.

"What a kiss, indeed. We should go, though. I'm afraid I can't kiss you for much longer and keep it PG-13."

He smiles that sweet smile at me. The one he has shown me every time I say something silly. The one he showed the kids at the hospital. I think this might be his genuine smile, and I feel like the luckiest girl in the world he has shown it to me.

I'M LYING IN BED, daydreaming about this man when I know I shouldn't. In a little over a week, this whole arrangement will be over and we will part ways. But what are the odds of me enjoying his company so much? It's been years since I spent this much time with anyone other than Hailey and had a good time. I don't know where that'd leave us, where that leaves me. Will we be friends or just a flash of a good time?

I work tomorrow but I'm off the next day, so I grab my phone and text him.

Me: Any plans for Friday?

Alex: Do you work?

Me: I'm off! Breakfast at Ronnie's?

Alex: Are you an early riser?

Me: I can be

Alex: Can you meet me at Ronnie's for the first breakfast? 5:00am

Me: Fuck, Alex. 5:00 am?!??!!?

Alex: It'll be worth it

Me: Fine, I'll see you there. You better order me coffee before I get there or I will die

Alex: You'll be fine

Me: Die

Me: Slow death

Me: Without caffeine

Alex: Ok Liv, see you Friday.

Me: Deal

FIVE DAYS BEFORE CHRISTMAS

On the fifth day of Christmas Baker Oaks gave to me a yoga class and kitchen shenanigans.

11

A RACCOON IN A
FIGHT WITH A HOSE
CALL IT WHAT YOU WANT, TAYLOR SWIFT

Livie

THIS SURELY WASN'T on my bingo card this year. Slow flow yoga at 6:00am with a retired football star? Nope. And not *regular* slow flow yoga, no. Slow flow yoga with a very sweaty, very hot, half-naked Alex. He ended up picking me up this morning because I didn't want to drive, and after a light breakfast at Ronnie's, we joined the 5:45am yoga class at Sunshine Flow, the local yoga studio. The class was good and I felt very in tune with myself and my body. At one point, I even teared up.

Alex, on the other hand? He was front and center, moving seamlessly with the instructor. I can tell he knows the flow by heart, because he looked like he was completely in sync with her. I've never in my life seen someone so broad and strong move like water—effortless and fluid. Halfway through the class, the studio got hot and he removed his shirt. Nobody even batted an eyelash, but me? I was a goner. I couldn't stop looking at the way his back flexed with every movement or the control in his arms and legs. Fuck, I'm no better than any man. I had to keep myself in check several times for the rest of the class.

When the class was over, some of the women gravitated toward Alex, like he was the sun and they were the planets orbiting around him. He was polite, with courteous nods and a shake of his head before excusing himself and coming to find me in the back corner.

"Hey Liv, you ready?" he asks, unaware of the effect he has on me. The effect he has on people in general.

"Yup. Let's go, Captain," I shout, walking out of the yoga place with zero chill. *Great, Livie, way to go.* I hop in his SUV and slam the door shut, tilting my head back on his seat and closing my eyes. *Maybe if I can't see it, it didn't happen.* I repeat to myself over and over again.

"Hey," Alex whispers in my ear and I shut my eyes even tighter. "I know better than to ask a woman if she's okay, but I don't know how else to ask."

"Yup. I'm fine. Dandy. Peachy," I bite, throwing a fit like a giant baby. So much for using my words and communicating just like I always said I would.

"Okay…since you're fine, dandy, and peachy, you wouldn't mind coming over to my house for a bit, right? I have some farm chores to do and could use some company," he says.

"Yup, I can."

We ride the rest of the way in silence. He doesn't live far away, so I knew it would be a quick drive, but what I didn't expect was how gorgeous his place is. I expected Alex to have more of a bachelor pad somewhere or even one of the newer fancy condos downtown. But no, his property is more of what Southern dreams are made of. We drive down a long L-shaped driveway framed by more live trees than I can count. Towering oaks arch gracefully overhead, their sprawling branches creating a beautifully green canopy that filters the sunlight, casting shadows on the gravel below. As we follow the road, it leads us to a charming white farmhouse, its crisp exterior standing in stark contrast to the greenery. Beside it is a cozy smaller house that looks like the twin of the main house, and Alex parks right in front.

"Wow," I let out in a breathy whisper.

"It's beautiful here, isn't it?" he asks as he looks around his property.

I nod. "It is." Alex hops out of the SUV and walks to my side to open the door, but I beat him to it and I'm already out. I feel so damn gross from yoga, all sweaty and shit while he still looks like a damn superhero.

"Agh, it's not even fair."

"What's not even fair?" he asks, confused by my little outburst.

"That you still look that good while I look like a smelly raccoon after getting into a fight with a hose."

Alex bursts out laughing and tries to cover it with his hand. "Liv, you don't look like a raccoon. And even if you tried to look like a raccoon, you would be the cutest raccoon there ever was. If you were uncomfortable, I could've dropped you off at home—you didn't have to come."

"Agh, I didn't even think about it!" I was in the middle of throwing my little fit back there and didn't stop to think. "I'm all wet and gross and a shower sounds about perfect."

"Then take one." He walks toward the front door of the smaller house. "I may not have strawberry soap, but I have some options."

"And what? Stay naked or put my dirty clothes back on?"

"I mean, naked sounds great." He winks at me before opening his door. When I don't go in, he takes a deep breath and says, "I'm kidding, Liv. You can wear some of my clothes while I wash yours, or I can just take you back home."

"No!" I shout, stomping into his house. *Very mature. Very cutesy, Livie.*

Alex places a hand on my forearm, stopping me before I

can get any farther. "Please tell me what's going on. I'm trying here, Liv, but you're not giving me much to work with. I thought you liked the yoga. You were doing great and looked so peaceful every time I looked back—and trust me, I looked. I'm not sure what went wrong here."

I rub my eyes with the heels of my hands. "You're going to think I'm insane."

"I won't. Come, let's talk. You want some water?" He's so calm as he holds my hands and guides me along the beautiful cinnamon-brown wooden floors and into his all-white kitchen. Tall ceilings, white furniture, and barely any pictures. Minimalistic, got it. His kitchen is pristine; not a single crumb anywhere and not a myriad of utensils lying on every surface like mine. It's picture-perfect in here. Of course, it is; he has zero flaws, so a perfectly clean house is on brand for sure.

"Do you even live here?" I ask while looking around, afraid to touch anything. He makes quick work of getting some water as I watch him move effortlessly like my heart doesn't skip a beat at the sight of this man. I'm wrapped in his perfect scent that happens to be everywhere here. He hands me a glass of water, foggy from the cold, as the condensation runs down my palm. I take a quick sip, letting the crisp water cool me off from the inside out, and set it down before hopping onto the countertop. Fuck, a habit I guess, but his house is so pristine and I'm beyond gross so I hop back down. "Sorry, sorry. I hope my sweaty ass didn't mess up your clean counters."

Alex walks to me, his eyes darkening with intention. He puts his glass down and wraps his arms around me. He leans down to grab my ass with both hands and whispers next to my ear, "The only thing your ass should make a mess of is my face, Livie. You can put that perfect ass of yours anywhere you want in this house, and it will be my greatest honor. Stop apologizing." He lifts me with his firm grip and places me back on the counter. His hands slide to my hips, and I shiver when he lets out a raspy breath right in my ear and murmurs, "You're so tense, Liv, and I'm not exactly sure what's happening—but I can help with part of it. If you'd let me, that is."

"You don't mean that. There's nobody around, though, no need for an act," I whisper. I shiver as he gets closer to me and I try to control how he's affecting me. With his damn Christmas cookie smell, even after a whole morning of yoga.

"Do you think *this* is an act?" he asks, tilting his hips forward so I can feel his hard dick on my leg. "Do you think that reaction is for people who might be watching us? Because let me answer that for you—it's not. It's because you've been driving me absolutely and completely fucking insane for the past seven days, and it's taking every ounce of chivalry I have not to bend you over and fuck you every time you pass by."

My breath hitches at his confession, my chest rising and falling rapidly and my hands frozen in place over his chest because *same, boy, same.* "Please bend me over and fuck me anytime you want, Alex," I whisper.

He got his permission. He got his consent, and he's not waiting a second longer to do something about it. Alex spreads my legs apart, sliding between them and grabbing my face with both hands. He hovers over my lips for a second, and when I don't feel his lips on mine, I open my eyes to find his gaze on me, pure molten lava. "Don't ask me for things you can't handle, shortie, because I will take your word for it and fuck you in this kitchen."

"I'm yours to do with as you wish. Kitchen or not," I whisper. He pulls my head to his and crashes his lips to mine. Not the tender careful kiss he usually begins with—this is a searing kiss. The kind that melts you from the inside out. I feel the embers rising from within as he kisses, licks, and pulls me close to him. He shoves my leggings and lace undies down, taking my shoes off and yanking the leggings off. Now my bare ass is on his cold and clean countertop, and here I was worried about my sweat. He opens my legs and drops his eyes to my center. I can see it in him; the heat, the desire, and it makes me feel so fucking alive I may combust just from the way he's looking at me.

"God, you're fucking perfect," Alex groans as he hooks his hands under the back of my knees and pulls me to the edge of the counter, spreading my legs even wider. His hand crawls up my leg, using his fingers to draw goosebumps all over me. *This is too much.* I'm so exposed in front of him and he doesn't seem to care, not one bit. The complete opposite, actually—he's so eager to touch and to watch what he's doing.

His thumb slides between my lips, finding my clit and pressing against it. The urge to close my legs at the sensation is strong, and almost as if he can hear my thoughts, he says, "Feet on the counter, Liv." He taps his other hand on my foot to raise it and fuck if this isn't both hot and obscene at the same time. He bites his lip as I'm spread wider right in front of his face. "Fucking perfect."

He positions his mouth right above my clit, replacing his thumb with his tongue and making my back arch. I moan as he licks my clit over and over again while he slides two fingers in. He pumps them in and out, keeping up with the same cadence of his tongue. I squirm under his touch, at the overwhelming feeling. It's so good, I don't know how long I'll last without coming all over his mouth.

He licks and sucks my clit hard as he slides three fingers in now, making me feel so full. "Fuck, Alex. Yes, just like that," I beg between moans and breathy sounds as he picks up the pace. I lift my hips to try to get more pressure on my clit, and when he bites gently, I see stars and burst into nothingness right in his mouth.

He groans against me, pumping his fingers slower now, allowing me time to come down from this perfect high. Once I'm in pure fucking bliss, Alex lowers my legs as he stands up and cradles my face, kissing me tenderly.

"You smell perfect and you taste perfect, too, Liv. Which heaven did you come from?" he asks against my lips, making me laugh loudly.

"What a dork," I add.

"Closeted hippie, grump, Thor of a man, and a dork. Anything else you would like to add to that list?" he asks, softly caressing my cheek. His eyes are glossy, full of desire.

"Nope, that about sums it up," I add, kissing him softly on his lips. "Sorry... I freaked out."

"About what?" he asks. And here's when I need to decide if I'm going to speak the truth or pretend like I'm not a crazy jealous person. I choose the first, because why the hell not? We're out here pretending to be together but that—what he just did—did not feel like we're pretending *anything*.

I let out a heavy breath and reply, "I didn't like sharing you with other women."

Alex raises an eyebrow. "Who did you share me with, Liv?"

"All those girls drooling over you at the yoga studio. I know I'm not really your girlfriend, but I still didn't like it."

"Were you jealous?" I bite my lip and nod—I need to be honest with him.

Alex smiles warmly at me before kissing my forehead. "Come on; let me show you where the shower is and I'll throw your clothes in the washer. Take your time—I have to go feed the animals but I'll be back."

"Are you not going to take care of that?" I ask. His dick looks like it's ready to break his pants and spring free.

He chuckles, shaking his head. "Nah, we can deal with this later. You can relax for a bit." He pulls me down from the counter and without dropping my hand, brings me to his bathroom, leaving me in there to shower.

12

____

FILTHY, FILTHY GIRL
DIVE DEEP (HUSHED), ANDREW BELL

ALEX

I WALK INSIDE after feeding the animals and telling my mom I have someone over. We usually have coffee together mid-morning, and I didn't want her to think I abandoned her today. She didn't ask lots of questions and just said to have fun.

I'm hoping Livie is done so I can hop in the shower real quick and see if she'd like to spend the day together. I'd be happy to spend the day doing whatever she wants as long as I can spend it with her.

"Liv," I call, knocking on the door to my bedroom. There's no answer from the other side. I push the door open and after I step into the sunlit room, I see there's a beautiful girl, wrapped in a towel on top of my bed and sleeping. I smile to myself at the sight. I grab my phone from my pocket, get closer to her, and snap a picture. You can't see anything other than her shoulders and her half-dried hair splayed across my navy comforter. The angle highlights her profile and her

85

closed eyes. Her eyelashes kiss the top of her cheeks and she looks so at peace.

I upload the picture to my stories with the caption "My little holiday gift," and put the phone down. I cover her soft curves with the blanket and back away to go shower. I hope the mix of quiet and steam helps me figure out how I'm going to let Livie know I might be falling in love with her, no matter how soon it may seem.

"GOOD MORNING, SHORTIE," I say to Livie, who finally rolls to her back. She's been sleeping for three hours, and I don't blame her. She woke up so early today and had a workout. Well, two workouts. I'm sure she's tired, so I just let her rest. I answered some emails and RSVPed yes to an event on Sunday with the hope she'll come with me. It's a benefit gala for the women's shelter in Jacksonville. I've been wanting to organize some drives and activities with them, but it's hard for them to trust a man who the media portrayed as a player.

"Three times, Alex. I've fallen asleep near you three times in the week we've been hanging out together. How is that even possible?" she groans, rubbing the sleep from her eyes.

"It's my comforting presence," I joke and she lifts her hand to her forehead, making her towel come undone. Her breasts peek out from where they were hiding, but she's still mostly covered. All I want to do is pull the covers down, to reveal all the curves hiding underneath.

"No, I think it's your cookie scent. Makes me feel like Christmas morning wrapped in a blanket." She pulls herself up to her elbows, the towel shifting more and making all my Christmas wishes come true with that sudden movement.

"What cookie scent?" I ask, getting up from the low chair I was sitting on. Her body is in full display and she hasn't attempted to cover herself, so I use that to my advantage and look shamelessly.

"You, your house, your sheets—all of it smells like a Christmas morning baking session. You say I smell like strawberries? Well, you smell like a blanket and warm cookies. Like the best hug on a busy day. Agh, it's not fair."

I chuckle at that and climb onto the bed. Livie scoots back, raising to her elbows and looking at me sheepishly. "This—" she adds, waving her hand and pointing to me "—is not fair either."

"What's not fair, shortie? That I want to devour you whole the minute I look at you, or that you're not only the sexiest woman I've ever seen but somehow also the cutest?"

Livie giggles. "It's not fair that you smell like that while looking like this, and on top of that, you're kind and funny. And a damn good listener, too."

"You forgot good in bed." I cage her body with mine and kiss her softly on her lips. I let my eyes roam her body slowly, and when I finally reach her face, I wink and smirk, pulling an eye roll from her.

"Cocky, too. That's what I should have said. You have something to back up that statement, Alex?"

"I have two or three tricks up my sleeve." I crash my mouth to hers, kissing her and holding nothing back. I kiss her soft plump lips and once they're swollen and perfect, I kiss her jaw, her earlobe, and her neck. I kiss and lick right above her collarbone until she's a writhing mess under me. ⊟

I cup one of her perfectly round breasts, so full and needy for attention. Her body is a damn masterpiece. All soft curves and sized to fit my hands, my mouth, and my dick to perfection. I haven't been able to keep our night in the SUV out of my mind. "I've been dying to be inside of you again, Liv. I can't wait to bury myself in your perfect little cunt."

She lets out a gasp as she hooks her legs and around my

hips. "Then do it, Alex. Fill every inch of me up with your dick."

"Liv, is your sweet little cunt needy for my dick?" I rasp and her eyes flare with fire.

"So needy for you, and *you* have too many clothes on." She bites her lower lip and moves to touch her clit. "I can touch myself if you need a little bit more time to get ready."

"Such a sassy little brat you are. Hands up." When she follows my command, I yank both of hers above her head. Pinning her hands down, my mouth lowers over her hard brown nipple.

"Mmm, yes," she whispers, arching her back and pressing harder into my mouth.

I continue kissing her from her breast all the way to her pelvis, a perfect trail of lust and desire. "God, your body is so perfect, Liv. So fucking perfect." She shivers under me in response to the praise. When I reach her center, I open her lips up with my finger, bringing my tongue right over her clit and licking her slowly.

"Fuck," she moans, this time louder than before as she wiggles under me, trying to get free from my grip.

I chuckle against her clit. "Oh, no, no—you said you were needy. This is me giving you what you need." I start again, kissing and teasing her until her whole body is tensing. I know she's almost there, but before she can come, I stop.

"What in the world, Alex?!" Liv shouts, her legs falling limp as she tries to free her hands again.

"You said you were needy for my dick. I was just getting you ready for it," I say with a triumphant grin as I pull my pants down with my free hand.

"I thought you said you weren't an asshole, Alex."

"It'll be worth it, I promise. Now lift your ass for me, Liv, and don't move your hands." I drop her hands for a minute, so I can grab a pillow to slide under her. With this new angle, I can see all of her open wide just for me. I stroke my dick once, feeling the precum right on my tip and sliding it down to the base of my dick.

"You're so hot, Liv, look what you do to me." When she sees how hard I am for her, I see her pussy clench. "You like that, Livie girl? Do you like knowing what you and your perfect body do to me? I'm so fucking hard it hurts. Are you ready to take me like the good girl you are?"

"God yes, please fuck me already."

I reach over to my nightstand, grab a condom, and open it up with my teeth. I slide it over my dick as Livie watches my every movement. I grab one of her legs and place her foot on my shoulder, giving me the perfect angle to slide into her and reach that spot I know will make her shiver instantly.

"Oh fuck," she moans. When I reach my hand back up to where her hands were waiting, still crossed over her head, I feel like the luckiest man alive.

"Good fucking girl, Liv. Not moving your greedy hands like I told you. You know what happens to girls who listen?" I ask, knowing damn well she can't form words with me touching her like this. With me talking to her like this. "They get rewarded." I slam into her hard, touching that spot again and earning me another moan.

"You like it when I talk dirty to you? My filthy, filthy girl? It's like you were made for me."

"Alex," she cries, breathy and unraveled.

"Come for me, Liv. Let me feel this perfect little cunt tighten around my cock."

She bursts around me, and it's the prettiest sight I've ever seen. She doesn't come moaning or shouting my name. No; she closes her gorgeous brown eyes and lets out a silent breath with her pretty, plump, and swollen lips slightly open. Her fingertips graze over my hands, digging her nails in and lifting her hips higher to reach the exact spot she wants. Her coming undone so gracefully under my body, with my dick deep inside of her, makes me lose control. With another pump surrounded by her warmth, I follow her and lose all my bearings, too.

I let go of her hands so I brace and bring my elbows on the bed, careful not to collapse over her. I bring my forehead to hers, evening out my breaths as I say, "That was…"

"Perfect," Livie finishes my thought. "That was perfect."

I lay down next to her, both of our chests rising and falling, and I close my eyes—wondering how the fuck am I going to let her go in five days.

THREE DAYS BEFORE CHRISTMAS

On the third day of Christmas Baker Oaks gave to me two idiots falling in love.

13

ALL I WANT FOR CHRISTMAS

ALL I WANT FOR CHRISTMAS IS YOU, GLEE CAST

LIVIE

> Hailey: I need a picture. I'm so mad I had to work tonight and I don't get to see your hot-ass-self waiting for your dream man. I'm so jealous. Does he have any single friends?

> Me: From what I gathered the other day, no. One is in a complicated relationship with his ex, another one has been hooking up with the same girl for years, and the other one has been married to his high school sweetheart all his life.

> Hailey: Boo! Ok then. Well still, I need a pic.

I STAND in front of the mirror and snap a picture of myself. I'm wearing an emerald green gown, completely fitted to my body. It has long sleeves covering my arms, and a deep V showing all the cleavage. It also has the perfect slit over my left thigh up to my hip. It's stunning and I knew I needed it the moment I first saw it. It has been hanging in my closet for years, waiting for the perfect occasion. What better occasion than being invited to the Gala for The Hubbard House?

The Hubbard House is a local shelter and foundation for victims of domestic violence. They have a full-service support hotline to help women and children escaping their abuser. My hospital works hand in hand with them, especially the trauma department where Hailey works. Their biggest fundraiser of the year is this Christmas gala. I've always wanted to go, especially because a lot of previous victims speak up about their journey and how everyone can help, even if it's not in a monetary way. I've never been able to attend because the tables are by invite only, and even then you have to pay thousands of dollars for the fee. So, when Alex said he was invited and that he's also been wanting to go for a while, I crossed my fingers and hoped he would ask me to go. Turns out, I didn't have to hope very hard because he wanted be his date. He was worried I was going to say no due to the short notice and needing a formal gown. Good thing I'm always prepared for a party.

Hailey: God, you look stunning. Such a shame I like dick so much because you're a damn smoke show, Livie.

Me: Thanks babe! I feel like a queen

Hailey: As you should. Have so much fun and take pictures. Also, I would love to see a picture of your man, too

Me: Not my man, remember? In three days, this whole arrangement is over and we're both going our merry ways.

Hailey: Not even a priest at a confessional would believe that, Livie. Have you seen the way he looks at you? I gotta go. Please send me pics

Hailey: Love you

Have you seen the way he looks at you? Yes, I fucking have and it doesn't make me feel any better. All I do is think over and over again about how we have this dumb arrangement and I couldn't keep my end of it. At no point did we talk about feelings. Because what were the odds that we would fall in love with each other in less than two weeks? If I'm being honest with myself, I don't know if I can call this love, but what is this feeling if I can't? Because when Alex looks at me, it's like my soul is on fire. And the only choice I have is to let it burn. When I spend time with him it's like every cell in my body is made of happiness, giddiness, and lust. When I'm with him, it's like I can barely even breathe unless I'm touching him. Unless I am kissing him. This isn't healthy, I know, but what am I supposed to do?

I grab my favorite lipstick from the countertop, a shade of maroon that makes my eyes look chestnut brown and my cheeks glow. It's matte and kissable, my favorite kind. It won't move from my lips no matter what I do and I kind of like that.

The doorbell rings, so I grab my black clutch and walk to the door to let Alex in. My hands are sweaty and my steps falter at the thought of seeing how he'll look in a suit and tie. He's so damn handsome. No matter what he wears, he looks edible. But there's just something about men in formal attire that gets me every time.

I open the door and I wish I could see my face because, oh, how wrong I was. If I thought picturing Alex in a suit and tie was hot, this scene in front of me is even more. Alex is standing at my front door in a navy blue bespoke tuxedo. The fabric is perfectly molded to every inch of his hard body, and the damn bowtie framing his neck is making me squirm. But that's not what stops me dead in my tracks. Alex's beautiful hazel eyes sparkle, freezing me in place. And to top it off, I notice he's holding a bouquet of beautiful roses when he flashes me his million-dollar smile.

"If I knew I was going to get that reaction out of you, I would've shaved a lot sooner," he jokes and I'm at a loss for words. I feel so freaking shallow it's unreal, but how is he God's favorite in every sense of the word? When God was giving away gifts, he must have run to the front of the line. Pretty eyes? First in line. Good height and body? First in line. A good sense of humor? First in line. Good in bed? First in line. A good listener? Agh! Everything. He was first in line for everything. I can't believe he's been single this long.

"Hi," I say, taking the flowers from his hand. "These are beautiful, thank you."

"Those aren't for you, though," he jokes.

"Oh, so funny," I laugh sarcastically. "Come on in, let me put these in water real quick."

After I get a vase from under the kitchen sink and add the flowers to it, I turn my body to look at Alex. I find his eyes on me with a giant smile on his face.

"Hi," I repeat.

"You said that already," he replies.

"I forgot words apparently."

Alex chuckles and grabs my hand, bringing it to his mouth and kissing it softly. "You look stunning, by the way. If I wasn't still standing and talking to you, I would think my heart stopped when you opened the door."

I'm sure I blush because his intense stare is still on me and I'm having way too many feelings. I don't know how I'm going to hold them back all night, or on Christmas Eve for that matter, because all I want to do is burst out with, *I think I'm falling in love with you and it's crazy, but it's true.* I don't say that, though; all I do is tuck a piece of my wavy hair behind my ear and reply, "Thank you. You don't look so bad yourself."

"Come on, Liv. Let's get to this gala so I can show you off."

I wrap my arm around his, and together we walk out of my house and to his SUV. I usually don't expect gifts on Christmas Day, but I find myself closing my eyes and wishing for one this year. Like that freaking hit song—all I want for Christmas is him.

14

CAN'T TAKE IT BACK
WINTER WONDERLAND, MICHAEL BUBLÉ

ALEX

"ARE YOU HAVING FUN?" I ask Livie while we're slow dancing. We've been at the gala for hours now. We had a delicious dinner and participated in the auction. I bid on some items, but the only two I won were an egg holder for my mom's kitchen—it matches her decor perfectly—and a ridiculous teddy bear Livie said would be a perfect Christmas gift for Laurie. She said Laurie acts all grown but she's a sucker for teddy bears, and Livie would love to bring her a giant one for her to snuggle with on the hard days of her treatment. I donated a signed football and I was shocked at how many people bid on it. At the end, it went to a couple who came to say hello in person. Apparently, I'm their son's favorite player and he was heartbroken when I retired. We made plans for me to hang out with their son soon, and they left with giant smiles on their faces.

"It's been an incredible night, Alex. I know you said people think you're an ass, but really people love you." She has her head laying on my chest and her chin tilted up to look at me.

"I think it's the Livie effect—people are usually not this nice to me."

"Oh, stop, is it the Livie effect or is it the fact you've been smiling all night? You're so damn good looking Alex that you're intimidating as fuck until you smile. I can guarantee that's why people didn't approach you before."

"So, the Livie effect indeed."

"What on earth, boy?"

"I only smile this much when I'm around you. So, yes, the Livie effect." We continue swaying to the soft piano rendition of "Rockin' Around the Christmas Tree."

"I want to talk about something," I tell Livie. I'm hoping that since we're in public, I can muster up the courage to tell her what I'm feeling for her. I don't want to scare her off, obviously, but I think I need to tell her how much I love spending time with her and that I would love to continue this past Christmas Day.

Before I can say anything, she replies, "I know, I know. We need to make a plan for Christmas Eve. My mom is already asking a million questions and I really need to prepare you for it. I need her to believe this is real so she can back off and I can go back to my life. We should hang out tomorrow after my shift so I can give you the rundown of things."

So I can go back to my life. I guess she doesn't feel the same way. I thought for a moment that I saw the same things in her eyes that I'm sure mine are showing, but I guess I was wrong. Maybe where I thought I was seeing love, all I was seeing was lust.

"Yes, that sounds like a plan," I reply in a clipped voice.

"I'm sorry I dragged you into this, but it's almost over. At least, on your side, things seem to be looking up, right?" Livie asks as she lifts her head from my chest. Her eyes are searching for something in mine, and I wish I could just be brave and tell her: that while social media-wise they are looking up if she disappears from my life in three days, things will be anything but fine.

"You didn't drag me, shortie. I offered," I say.

"You know, I always assumed you called me shortie because I'm short. But I've been meaning to ask if there was another reason," she offers, biting her lower lip with a half-smile on her face.

"Remember when I said you smell like strawberries?" I ask and she nods. "You remind me of Strawberry Shortcake. Sweet, cute, vibrant, and you smell like it, too. So yeah, my little shortcake."

"You're such a dork," she teases, lowering her eyes and smiling to herself.

"We've established that already."

The song ends and we walk back to our seats. Livie takes a sip of her red wine and I wish I could say I do something other than stare at her but I can't. I'm a goner and in so much trouble. I need to figure out a way to be okay when the arrangement is over, but at this rate, I'm not sure it will happen.

"Do you want to go see what desserts they're hiding in the kitchen?" she asks.

"What? No, we already had dessert," I reply with confusion.

"Yeah, but they always have good ones in hotel kitchens. Come on, let's see what we can find." Livie stands up, leaving her purse and her phone on top of the table, and I follow right behind her. She moves with ease through the hallways, pulling me behind her until we cross a door that says Staff Only. She keeps walking like she owns the place and nobody bats an eyelash at either of us. At the end of the dimly lit room, there are some silver double doors. She pushes through them and even though it's pitch black, she keeps walking.

"Livie!" I say in half a whisper, half a shout.

"Shh, shh, come on. I've been here before. Don't ask why, or how I know, but we're almost there." She hits something with her hip and shouts, "Fuck!" while stopping for a second before continuing.

"Are you okay?" I ask, not letting go of her hand but getting close to stopping her because this is crazy.

"Yeah, just a bump on the hip. Here, this way," she directs, as she pulls me toward the small door at the back with light shining through a little window. She rattles the handle and after a hard yank, she opens the door. She pulls us both through and now we're in the middle of what looks like an industrial pantry. No, not a pantry—more like a mix between a fridge and a pantry. It's slightly cold on one side, but where we're standing there are some boxes and shelf-stable items.

"Come on, this way." She drops my hand and walks toward the back where there's another door and when she opens it, she gasps and says, "Score!"

I look up and see a selection of cakes, pies, and other desserts. She shoves half her body into the fridge, shuffling things around and mumbling something under her breath.

"Livie, is this even legal?" I ask, trying to contain my laughter at the sight in front of me.

"No, but who's gonna know? Also, all these get thrown away after twenty-four hours. I highly doubt someone's going to order all of these late into the night. AHA! Look!" she shouts, pulling a heart-shaped cake decorated with strawberries out of the fridge.

My jaw drops. "Is that…"

"Strawberry shortcake!" Livie shouts again. "Look! Look! It's either that, or strawberry cheesecake, but either works." She walks past me, setting the cake on the counter and opening some cabinets until she finds two measuring spoons. She hands me one and when I look at her suspiciously, she says, "Listen, this is the only thing I could find. But we will wash it before we're done, okay?"

She dips the measuring spoon into the corner of the cake and after she scoops a piece out, she says, "Strawberry short-cake, indeed—it's your lucky day."

"You're unbelievable," I say, and I mean it in the most magical way. Like… where did she come from and how did I manage to cross paths with her?

"Unbelievably cute, right?"

"That for sure. Also, unbelievably amazing."

She blushes at the compliment, taking a giant bite of the cake. She opens her mouth to say something but realizes she can't chew and talk so she rolls her eyes at herself. I smile, taking a bite of my own and basking in this moment. Basking in the silence and her company.

Once she swallows, Livie immediately starts talking. "I don't get it. You're near perfect; why has nobody snatched you up? You say all the right things, do all the right things, look like that, and I'm pretty sure you're a mama's boy, too. You're such a gentleman that there's no way your mother didn't have a say in that. I'm pretty sure she's the one who lives in the bigger house back at your place, right?"

She's observant and I like it. I could choose to avoid this conversation and try to get away with some bullshit excuse, but I choose bravery and tell her the truth. "My mom raised me all by herself. My dad—if you can even call him that—left her when she was pregnant with me. At just eighteen years old, she had to learn how to be an adult and raise a baby on her own. She worked endless odd jobs until I was old enough to go to school, and then she tried to work around my school schedule so she could still spend time with me. When I turned seven and made the Pop Warner football team, Mom smiled so big, it could've lit up the whole town. That night I heard her crying on the phone to her friend about how she didn't know how she was going to pay for everything." I take another small bite, letting the sweet taste of the cake bring me back to this moment and not to the memory I'm sharing. Livie stops looking at the cake and keeps her eyes on me, attentive to every word I say.

"I tried selling my clothes at school to help pay for stuff. And when the principal called my mom to tell her, she cried again. I was only eight years old but I felt awful because now she had cried not once, but twice, because of me. She always said that boys should bring girls flowers and smiles and no tears, so why was I bringing tears to my mom? When we got home that night, I told her I didn't really like football that much, and that I'd rather do homework on the floor at her job than play. She saw right through my bullshit, of course, and what she did instead was call everyone she knew in town to see if they could sponsor me. Little did she know, Pop Warner offered scholarships, and one of the people she asked about sponsorship moved some things around and I was awarded a full one. It included everything, even transportation from school to practice. I refused to go until she told me. And after I found out I was so grateful that I never messed up. Not once." I put the spoon down and slide to the floor, sitting with my back against the counter and my legs up. I was always told I looked like a mountain sitting like this, but I don't really care because it's so comfortable.

Livie grabs the cake and slides down next to me, laying her head on my shoulder. She stays silent, not knowing that her presence is so comforting, I don't feel like I need to hide this from her.

"I studied and I did good in school and I played my heart out on the field. I wasn't good, but I was dedicated. I had good sportsmanship and grit. It's truly all you need to be good at anything. I was a little delusional, too, and I kept shooting for a shot at a college ball scholarship and hopefully helping my mom out someday. One thing led to another, and I ended up being drafted. What a wild ride it was. I always promised myself that the first thing I would do if I had a lot of money would be to get my mom the house she always wanted and make it so she could retire. She let me build the house, but she likes working, so she still does. Her dream house was a farm, so I made it happen. And she always said she wanted me nearby, so when one day I gave her grandchildren, they wouldn't be far. I built the in-law suite, not knowing it would become my sanctuary the past few years."

"Okay, so I was right—you are perfect," Livie whispers, wiping a tear off of her cheek. "I still don't get it."

"Well Liv, you know what happens when you lose your goals? Or, in my case, when you achieve them? I lost my north. So here I was, a professional football player with more money than I could count, and not knowing what the fuck to do. I felt so hollow and so empty. I decided partying was the way to fill my heart. Plot twist—it didn't, it just drove me into a deeper hole. One harder to get out. So you see, sweet Livie, no matter how good-looking you are, how much money you have, or how good you are deep down… if you treat people like shit, they eventually leave you alone. The only reason I have friends is because my high school friends never gave up on me, even when I pushed them away."

Livie takes my hand, puts it in her lap, and starts drawing small circles on the back. Letting me know she's here and she's listening.

"The only thing I didn't play around with were drugs because I knew they could end my career. But everything else was fair game. And God, now that I know better, I wish I could take it all back. I hurt so many people, Liv. So many." I take a deep breath and continue because if I don't, I might never tell her. "The day I got injured, my coach gave me an ultimatum. I didn't even start the game because of how fucked up I'd been in the game before. But the starting quarterback had a family emergency and left at halftime so I took his place. I didn't even complete one play when someone hit me from the side at just the right angle that my femur snapped. I could see the bone almost pushing through. And, well, I already told you about the rest. I was messed up badly, and to add the injury to it, it was too much. I really didn't want to live anymore, let alone try to get better. It took an intervention and my mom begging me to literally do anything to try and save her son. That's what did it. I committed myself to an inpatient mental health facility. There, I met my therapist and found yoga. And here I am a few years later. I still need work, which is why I attend both yoga and therapy religiously. And, well, being in a relationship with someone just has not been in the plans. I needed to heal first before I dragged someone else down with me."

Time moves both slowly and fast at the same time. I feel my heart beat faster than usual, but with Livie's eyes on mine, I feel like we're suspended in the moment. "No taking it back now."

"What?" she asks between sniffles.

"Calling me perfect, you can't take it back." I smile at her, trying to keep this moment light after the whole trauma dump.

"I could never take it back, especially after you shared that with me. You're so perfect, Alex. And the girl who gets to keep you will be the luckiest girl in the world," she assures me with tears in her eyes.

I open my mouth to say something, but the door snaps open behind us and a security guard from the hotel walks through it. Livie lifts her hands and says, "Oop!" while the guard shakes his head and asks us to follow him.

ONE DAY BEFORE CHRISTMAS

On the day before Christmas, Baker Oaks gave to me a book boyfriend standing in front of me.

15

BOOK BOYFRIEND LINES
WEIGHT, ALEXZ JOHNSON

LIVIE

Ma: Olivia, can you bring bread with you?

> Me: Yup, what kind?

Ma: Telera mija.

> Me: Mom, where am I supposed to find Telera, an hour before I'm supposed to be at your place.

Ma: You're a smart girl. Figure it out

Mateo: I have Telera at home, I'll bring some

> Me: Thanks, Matty.

Ma: Always saving your sister. Such a good big brother. I'll see everyone here

I SWIPE out of our family chat and text my brother

separately. I haven't even made it to dinner and I'm already on edge.

> Me: Thank you!

> Mateo: Don't let this bother you, O. You know how she is sometimes. I can't wait to see you and that boyfriend of yours

> Me: Thanks, Matty. Are you bringing anyone this year?

> Mateo: Just Daisy as usual.

> Me: EEEEEEEEH! I love me some Daisy! See you in a few

I love Mateo, my protective older brother. He is also single as fuck, but my mom doesn't care, because in her culture men can take whatever time they want to have a family. But women were made for one purpose—to get married and have children, nothing else. I don't have anything against either of those things, but the reality is that everyone's timing looks different. And honestly, I'm tired of letting her dictate my worth by whether or not I decide to push a baby out of my vagina. She's my mom and I don't want to let her down, but I also need her to get a grip.

I hear Alex's SUV engine and I open the door before he has a chance to ring the doorbell. Without saying hi, I turn back to the living room to grab all the bags with gifts I've had in a pile for weeks. My family usually exchanges gifts on Three Kings Day, but I'm always working then, so I bring their presents on Noche Buena.

"You look like an elf tonight, shortie," Alex calls from somewhere in front of me, but I can't see him behind the tower of presents I'm carrying.

"What, green and tiny?" I ask.

"More like cheerful with arms full of gifts. Here, let me

help you." He takes all the gifts from me and he's still able to stand up straight as if it doesn't bother him one bit.

"Agh, you have perfect hands, too. Not fair."

"So, I can carry you better," he replies, winking at me.

"Also, why are you wearing a suit? Not complaining, I love the view, but that's a little too formal." And that I do. He looks more than handsome with a dark green suit and his pretty smile.

"You said your mom's an etiquette freak, and she keeps setting you up with people with corporate jobs. I'm not giving her any indications that I'm not perfect for her daughter, so a suit it is."

"I swear if you keep saying shit like that, I'm going to have to keep you forever, Alex." *Great, Livie. Smooth, Livie. Not scaring him off at all, Livie.* He doesn't say anything and just walks out to put the gifts in his SUV. I grab the two bags I had by the door and follow him out. I've been thinking about how on earth I'm going to let him know I don't want this to end tomorrow without scaring him off. But God, that man can have anyone he wants, and I just don't know if he wants that one to be me.

"Ready for your quiz?" I ask as Alex follows the GPS to my mom's house. We are about an hour and a half away. So we have plenty of time to prepare for what's about to happen in that house.

"Your mom's name is Ada and your dad's name is Omar. They grew up near each other and moved to Florida soon after they got married. Your mom's a stay-at-home wife and she raised you and your brother Mateo. Mateo lives in Magnolia Springs, not too far away from your parents, and although you're all adults, your mom likes to stick her nose in y'all's business. She's allergic to pollen, which is why I don't have any flowers with me, and they like baseball more than football, so they won't be fans."

"You get an A."

"Not an A plus?" he asks nonchalantly.

"Alex, this is serious. I don't want your night to be miserable." My brother and my dad will be fine. Daisy—Mateo's best friend—is a sweetheart. too. So, really, all I have to worry about is my mom hurting his feelings or making him run for the hills. If I'm going to be successful with this charade, or if I'm brave enough to see if he's willing to date me after tomorrow, I need him to get along with her. Or at least not think I'm crazy and not want to spend more time with me.

"Liv, it will be fine. I won't be miserable, especially if I'm spending time with you."

"Why do you always know what to say?" I ask.

"I read a lot of smut," he replies.

Wait. "Wait what?"

"What, what?"

"You read romance?" I ask, opening my eyes so wide it feels like they might pop out.

"Why is that so hard to believe? And if you tell me some stereotypical shit, I'm calling you out on it."

"Alright, alright. Yes, I was going to say some *men don't read romance* bullshit but I'm actually surprised. Why didn't you tell me?"

"Why didn't you ask?" His expression is nonchalant as he pulls up by my mother's house right behind my brother's fancy ass car. Mateo works for the local hockey team, and he's a big deal. He's the owner's right-hand man, so he does more than anyone actually knows. He loves it, and it allows him to live a fancy lifestyle that otherwise he wouldn't be able to afford. It's just funny to me how our parents are huge baseball fans. There's a baseball team in Magnolia Springs, but Mateo decided to go work for the hockey team instead.

"I don't know. I've never dated anyone who reads books, so I never thought to ask," I reply, realizing that I just implied I'm dating him. I know technically I am, but for all intents and purposes, we're really not. *Then why do we kiss and fuck when we're alone?* the little voice inside my head harps. Lust and forced proximity are the answers I keep coming back to. *Oh. My. God. How many tropes have we been in?*

"Then it sounds to me like you're dating the wrong people. I love reading, and reading romance has been good for me and my soul, Liv. I can explore so many themes while having the safety net that, no matter the story, the couple will get their happily ever after. It's the closest thing to magic there is out there and I will die on that hill."

"Alex Haddock, you're speaking book boyfriend lines," I add.

"The highest compliment one could ever give me."

I'm done for. Officially ruined by this man. I don't think there will ever be anyone who could compare to him, and I either need to figure out how to keep him forever or how to fucking clone him.

DINNER GOES BY PRETTY FAST. *Seamlessly* fast. It was uneventful, or at least as uneventful as it could be, considering it's my mother we're talking about. She asked Alex all the questions I assumed she would ask and he answered them with flying colors. He asked a few questions about the food and tried everything. He even gave her a few compliments. He said some words in Spanish which is more than they get from me. I can understand Spanish, with no issues. I can listen to music in Spanish too and enjoy it. But I hate speaking it. I grew up feeling like I wasn't Latina enough because I didn't speak the language or because of my accent, so I just stopped trying. But the older I get, the more I realize that there's not a one box fits all and I am Latina. Even if I choose not to speak Spanish with others. I'm proud of my culture and happy my parents took the time to teach us. Maybe one day I will feel comfortable enough to speak it with my family, but in the meantime, I'm fine replying to my parents in English. The amount of Spanish I speak does not determine my ethnicity and I've made my peace with that.

We're sitting in the living room, talking and sharing some ideas for New Year's Eve, which is the other dinner my parents host. I usually miss that one and nobody even bats an eye. But my mother still makes sure I have my twelve grapes ready to wish for prosperity as the clock strikes midnight and my suitcase to run around so I get more traveling in my life. Both are traditions she loves and she's series about passing them on.

I'm sipping on Ponche when Alex brings me a piece of flan from the kitchen.

"Mm, there was some extra?" I ask.

"Yeah, you said that was your favorite, right? I hope your mom doesn't mind," he adds, looking at her.

She closes her lips in a flat fake smile that we can all see right through and says, "Oh darling, I made the flan for everyone. I just hope Olivia doesn't eat too much, in case her clothes won't fit her you know? We already know she could use it to lose some weight."

"Mom!" Mateo shouts.

"What? It's true. We could all be a little bit more mindful of how much sugar we eat, right?"

I want the earth to swallow me whole. The little jabs at my weight come and go, but I was hoping because Alex was here for the first time, she would back off. It was too much to wish for. She didn't make any comments about children so of course she had to make a comment about my weight.

"Mom, please," I beg.

"Oh, now I'm the villain, but when Olivia comes crying because her athlete of a boyfriend dumped her, you'll all know why."

"Mom!" Mateo shouts again.

"You're out of line," Alex barks before clearing his throat

and adding, "Respectfully, that is. I know I'm new here and this is your home, so the last thing I want to be is disrespectful. But ma'am, you've been making mean comments about your daughter all night. Some are a little bit more discreet than others but mean, nonetheless. Livie has been nothing but kind all night and this isn't fair to her. Your daughter is happy—isn't that what most parents wish their kids were? Happy? Not only is she happy, but she's such a light in so many people's lives, and that should be celebrated. However, I did not hear one single thing about it all night. Respectfully, her weight shouldn't be anyone's business but hers. What she eats, how she dresses, who she dates either. She is such a gift; girls like her are rare, and I honestly think you've forgotten how rare of a gem you have. Maybe it's time someone reminds you. I don't like the way you talk to her or about her, and nobody should put up with that. Would you say these things to a stranger? Would you say things like that to *me*?"

The room is completely quiet. You could hear a pin drop. My mom's mouth is open wide and my dad is sitting with his arms on his legs, not saying a word.

"Again, I'm sorry if I'm out of line, but enough is enough. Livie deserves better than this. You haven't even touched any of the gifts she brought or asked her any genuine questions. Instead, you want to make comments about her seemingly imperfect body? Because let me tell you, her body is perfect the way it is. I would know."

"Alex…" I whisper, looking at my dad, who's currently cringing right now.

"Sorry sir," he says. "Actually, sorry to you both," Alex continues. "The last thing I wanted to be was disrespectful in your home. But I care about your daughter, and I don't like hearing those words about her. Now if you'll excuse me," he adds, standing up and walking toward the back of the house.

"Olivia," my mom says, but before I can answer, my brother interrupts.

"He's not wrong, Mom. Let her go after him." Not that I needed her permission, but when she nods at me with tears in her eyes, I know she heard him. *Both* of them. I get up and follow Alex past the dining table, to the back door, and onto the porch.

16

___

I LOVE IT WHEN YOU CALL ME THAT
THE DOOR (STRIPPED), TEDDY SWIMS

ALEX

GREAT FUCKING JOB, Alex. It was going fine until you decided to yell at her parents. So much for winning them over so she has no choice but to keep you. Now you've fucked that up, too.

"Hey," Livie's soft voice echoes behind me.

"On a scale from one to ten, how much do you think your mom hates me right now?" I ask, not turning to see her. I'm so disgusted with myself but I couldn't stand there hearing her mom talk shit about her like that.

"Probably a seven, but you know what's more important than that?" she asks, curling her hands around my waist and hugging me from behind. The air outside is chilly and even though I'm not cold, I feel instantly warm with her arms around me.

"What? Because the whole reason I've been fake dating you is to get your mom off your back; now I'm guessing I just made it worse."

"More important right now is how much more I like you

117

because of what you just did back there." I hold her hands in mine and turn around to face her. Livie's arms are still wrapped around me and when I look down at her face, she's smiling softly at me even though tears are running down her cheeks. "No one has ever stood up for me like that, and you did it so respectfully. Her jabs don't affect me anymore; I've worked through healing the inner me and loving me the way I am. But still, having someone in my corner when she was being like that was beyond what I could have expected. Thank you," she whispers.

I bring my thumb up her face and wipe a tear from her cheek.

"I'm so sorry she talks to you that way, Liv. Nobody should have a say in what you eat, how much you eat, or your body for that matter. Unless it's to tell you how perfect your body is," I add. I cup her face, holding her in place so she has no choice but to look at me. "Do you hear me, Liv? Nobody. I'm sorry if I crossed the line, but I'm not sorry I spoke my mind."

She rises on her tiptoes and kisses me gently on the lips. "Thank you. That was the kindest thing anyone has ever done for me."

I grab her hands and pull her to sit on the swing hanging on the screened-in porch. She sits on my lap, her hands reaching for my face before kissing me again. She kisses me with care. She kisses me tenderly. Her lips are caressing mine and I've never felt this love before. I don't care what people might say: I love this girl, and I think she might love me back.

"Liv," I whisper against her lips.

"I love it when you call me that," she whispers back.

"I love calling you that, shortie."

"I love it when you call me that, too." We both laugh at that and continue kissing, exploring our lips, and getting tangled in each other. I'm sure plenty of time passes before we stop kissing. It's not the first time that the construct of time feels less of a reality than ever. Are there twenty-four hours in a day, and what is actually a day? Anyone who might hear this story might think I'm crazy falling in love with someone after eleven days—but I don't think I am. I could say that this feeling, this rush, is lust but I don't think it is. Lust is ephemeral and I don't think this feeling—this hug around my heart, this hold she has on me—is anything but love. Even if she doesn't feel the same way, I don't think there will ever be an 'after Livie' for me. I think there is *before her* and *after I met her*. Everything after will be either pure bliss with her or an eternal nightmare without her.

"I have something to tell you, Livie," I start.

"Me too, but you go first," she replies.

"You know this whole arrangement we have going on?" I ask.

"Yeah… it's coming to an end and I couldn't be more grateful for you coming with me today. Thank you so much. I know I was a mere stranger to you less than two weeks ago, and you've given me more than I asked for."

"You don't have to thank me, Livie, but please let me just say this one thing."

She looks up at me with her pretty doe eyes, but before I can begin to tell her how I feel, we hear the door opening. We look to the side and see her mom standing there.

"I'm so sorry to interrupt, but do you think there's any way I can talk to Livie?" she asks. When I look at Livie, her eyes widen and she slowly shakes her head no.

She turns to look at her mom and a couple of seconds pass before she says, "You know what, Mom? No; if you have something to say, you can say it in front of Alex, considering you just embarrassed me in front of him, too."

"Olivia, I didn't mean to embarrass you. I was just simply making a comment."

"An offensive comment, Mom. That wasn't cool and you not noticing is even worse." Livie lets out a sigh and presses her hand to her face before continuing, "Mom, the biggest problem is that it's not the first time you've said these things. You're so focused on my weight or who I date, but you've never heard *me* complain about any of the things *you* seem to be focusing on."

"I just want you to be happy, O."

"I am happy, Mom. That's the thing—I am truly happy. I love my life the way it is. I love my body the way it is. I love food, Mom. I don't want to spend the rest of my life on a diet to fit some social standard. You taught me to love myself above it all—but when did *you* stop loving me above it all?" she asks and her mom breaks into a soft sob.

"I love you, Mom, but your words are hurtful. And truly, if you want me to keep having a relationship with you, you need to work on that. Nobody likes going somewhere where they're never appreciated."

"I—" her mom starts, but Livie gets up from my lap and hugs her.

"It's okay, Mom. I know you mean well and I don't need you to say anything right now. I just need you to think about it, okay? We're going to go, but I'll call you tomorrow, okay?"

"Okay. I love you, Olivia," her mom replies against her neck.

"I love you too. Call me tomorrow," Livie insists before turning around to look at me. "You ready?" she asks and I nod, getting up from the swing and following behind her.

"Thank you for having me, Mrs. Sanz, I hope I get to see you again soon."

We say goodbye to the rest of her family and get in the SUV to head back to her place. "Can I ask for a favor?" Livie asks as we hit the long dark highway.

"Anything," I reply and I mean it. There's nothing I wouldn't give this girl, even if that means letting her go tomorrow.

"I know our deal ends tonight, I guess, but can I stay over at your place? We can end this tomorrow if you want, but I don't want to spend the night by myself. I know you spend Christmas morning with your mom and I don't want you to miss that, so can I just crash on your couch tonight?" She's biting her lower lip as her fingers shift, making small circles around with her thumbs.

"Liv, you can crash in my bed any time, no need for a couch. And let's talk tomorrow if you're talked out for today. Do you need clothes from home?"

"Do you mind stopping?"

"Not at all," I reply. If this means I get to spend an extra day with her, an extra minute, an extra second—so be it. Tomorrow though? Tomorrow, I fight for this. Tomorrow, I fight for her.

CHRISTMAS DAY

ON CHRISTMAS DAY Baker Oaks gave to me the love of my life wrapped under the tree.

17

———

THE GREATEST GIFT
SANTA TELL ME, ARIANA GRANDE

LIVIE

"MERRY CHRISTMAS, LIV," I hear a voice whisper in my ear. I open my eyes and see Alex sitting next to me on his bed where we spent the night exploring our bodies. If I didn't know better, I'd say his touch and his kisses all night were more a plea than a goodbye, but maybe I'm just hoping.

Twelve days. Twelve days is all it took for me to fall head over heels for the best man I've ever met. Twelve days and my silly, silly heart can't comprehend that this is ending today. I want to cry just thinking about it, but this was our deal and I'm going to be a big girl and deal with it. And by deal with it, I mean smile and nod when he tells me it was nice but then cry in a pint of ice cream tonight while watching Divergent for the eighth time in a row.

"Merry Christmas," I whisper, sitting up and covering my very naked body with the blanket. I ended up not needing any of the clothes I packed since he stripped me out of the red dress I wore last night. And to be honest, I was entirely too tired to fight him on the *you don't need clothes* moment before we went to sleep. We slept intertwined with each other and it was perfect.

"Coffee for you so you don't die a slow death," he teases, giving me a mug with a little cinnamon sprinkled on top of my coffee.

"You angel, I love this," I say, closing my eyes and taking a big whiff before taking a sip. "How's your mom?" I ask, knowing he was already over there for their morning routine.

"She's thankful for another Christmas together and she just left to spend some time with her friend," he answers, adding air quotes around the word 'friend.'

I chuckle and take another sip, letting this perfect cup of coffee warm up every inch of me. "So, what's your plan today?" I ask, secretly hoping that whatever it is, he can take me with him.

"It depends."

"It depends on what?"

"Here, why don't you put this shirt on and sit on the balcony with me?" he offers, handing me one of his shirts and opening up a blanket for me to step right into. I do as he says and when he wraps me up with the blanket, he leads the way to the balcony right outside of his room.

The balcony faces the vast greenery of his farm and some of the oaks, too. It's beautiful and peaceful out here. I can imagine myself sitting on this comfy chair, wrapped in a blanket with a book in hand.

Alex sits on the chair first, pulling me onto his lap and kissing my cheek gently. God, I'm going to miss these sweet kisses.

"Liv, I've been trying to tell you this for the past four days and it has been near impossible. So I do really need you to let me say it. If when I'm done you think I'm crazy, we can add that to the list of names you've called me. Is that okay?" he asks. Even though I want to ask so many questions, all I do is nod.

"I know we only met twelve days ago. I know that for most people, and on most occasions, that's not enough time to say someone has changed their lives. But I think that might not be the case here. You see, Livie, these past twelve days… I've laughed more than I have in years. I've smiled more, too. I know it may sound dumb but I've been trying to find how to give more meaning to my life, and I thought volunteering and fundraising events might give me that. And I'm sure they will, but to be honest, what has shown me that life is more than the daily grind and whatever other lies I've told myself… is you. I've enjoyed every single second I got to know you. I've more than enjoyed it. I don't know how I'm supposed to wake up tomorrow and not see you or talk to you. God, I don't even know how to say this other than I think I might love you, Liv. And I know it may sound crazy, but I do, and I would love nothing more than to show you for the rest of your days how much that's true."

I stay quiet, letting this moment sink in. He loves me. He loves me. He loves me. "Alex," I start.

He shakes his head, looking away from me. "It's okay, Livie. I just needed to let it out. The deal was until today, so I understand."

I can barely contain my grin. "No, you dummy! That wasn't a sad *Alex*, that was an *I can't believe this is happening, Alex*. What if I told you I love you, too, you big grumpy, closeted hippie, dork? I thought I was crazy, but apparently, I'm not. And we're both just two fools who fell in love with each other."

Alex lifts me up, pulling me closer to him and hugging me tight, spilling the coffee all over the floor. "God, I love you so much. Thank you," he says.

"Thank you for what?" I ask.

"Thank you for being you. Thank you for being the gift

rarely given this Christmas and thank you for letting me love you, Liv. I promise I will show you how you deserve to be loved every day for as long as you let me."

"I can't wait to show *you* how you deserve to be loved, too. Merry Christmas, Alexander James Haddock."

"Merry Christmas, my little elf."

EPILOGUE
MARRY YOU, BRUNO MARS

April

LIVIE

"THE MONSTER'S COMING," I growl, lifting my hands up, holding them like claws and chasing the kids into the lounge. This has been a hard month for all of us as we lost one of our nurses. More often than not, it's the children who either leave or sometimes unavoidably pass away. The latter is the saddest part of this career but we know that it will happen. Losing one of our nurses in a freak accident is not. I've tried my hardest to be present for the kids. Not only present, but happily present. Playing and reading to them every chance I get to try to alleviate some of the sad feelings floating around. The air has finally cleared and I feel like everyone is smiling again.

"Where are the children? I'm going to eat the children!" I call in a Scooby Doo villain's voice, but when I turn the corner and into the lounge, all the children are sitting or standing in a line. They're all looking at me with big smiles on their faces and holding pieces of paper.

"Mmm, what are you guys doing?" I question as I stand there confused. I look around and see some of the nurses, Cassie, Mateo and Hailey looking my way, all smiling too. "Okay, is someone going to explain to me what's going on?"

All the children start saying nonsense sounds but together it sounds like a funny melody. Almost as if they're trying to sing acapella for me. I clap on the beats of their voices, smiling at them because I will always be their greatest cheerleader. But this rhythm, this melody, is awfully familiar.

Zack, one of the boys, steps forward singing the first line of 'Marry Me' by Train. As he finishes it, he looks to the side, and then Laurie, our resident grump, steps forward and sings the following line.

"What's going on?" I ask as Lilly sings the next line, followed by her index finger going up to her mouth signaling me to be quiet. They keep going all the way to the end of the line. Riley, the last kiddo standing in the formation, turns his face to Zack at the same the song is about to go to the chorus. I would know, because this is one of my favorite songs in the world.

As the chorus starts, all the children, one by one, start flipping the papers.

"Will…" I whisper.

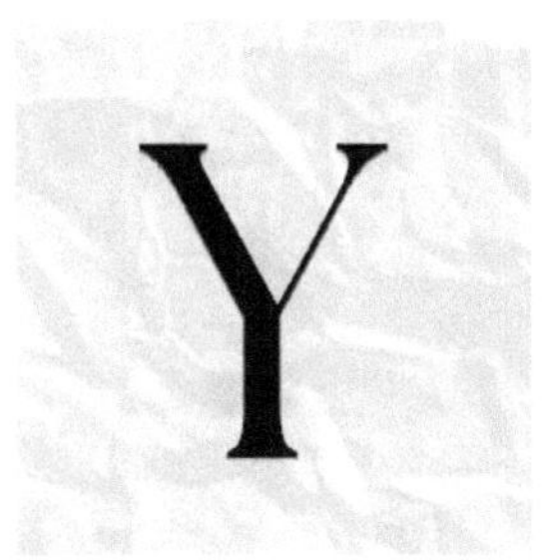

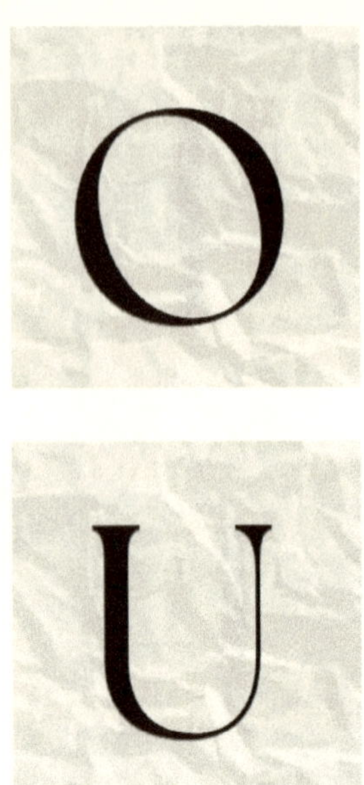

"You? Will you?" They start smiling bigger and Cassie's now crying. *What on earth?*

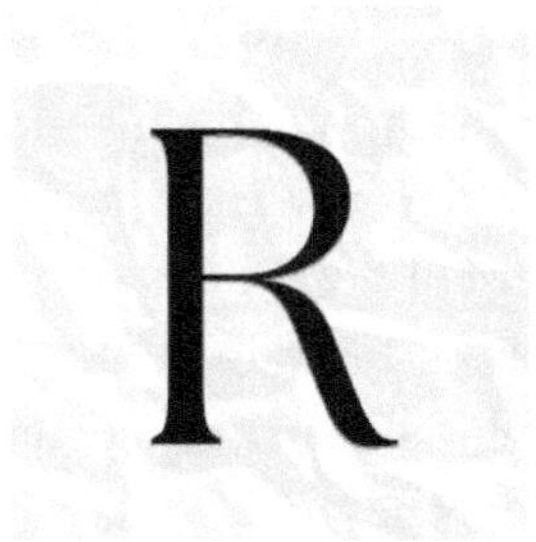

"Mare? Will you mar—" Oh my God. As soon as I try to read the last bit of the message, the last kids flip their papers, completing the question *Will you marry me?* They move to the side of the room, continuing their singing. There, in the middle of the hospital lounge, wearing the emerald green suit I love, is Alex on one knee.

I let out a sob, covering my mouth as I walk to him. He's flashing me his million-dollar smile, warming everyone in this cold room with it. He's singing the rest of the song, with his completely out-of-pitch tone that I love so much. He holds my hand with his left as his right hand is holding the most beautiful ring I've ever seen. It's a princess-cut solitaire diamond in a delicate gold band. *Classy and simple is all I want,* I told him in passing the other day when we were talking about celebrity rings. The sneaky, sneaky boy was probably asking for this purpose because this is exactly what I pictured when I said that.

"Alex, what are you doing?" I ask in between sobs.

"Asking the most beautiful girl, my best friend, my best comfort, and my best goodnight to make me the happiest man in the world and spend the rest of her life with me," he replies.

"And who's that?" I laugh, trying to sound nonchalant and not break down into ugly tears in front of him.

"You, Liv. I would love nothing more than to spend the rest of my life with you."

"Alex, we've only been together for a few months. This is crazy," I whisper, not dropping his hand.

"And? I don't need one more day to know I don't ever want to wake up without you by my side. I don't need one more week to know I never want to kiss anyone else—I never want to see anyone else. I don't need one more month to know that you're the best friend a man could ever ask for. I want to spend the rest of my life sharing my secrets, my goals, my days with you. I don't need one more year to know you're the best thing that has ever happened to me, Liv. Do you? Do you need more time?"

"No, you sweet summer child, I don't need more time," I whisper, throwing myself around him and hugging him tight."

"So, is that a yes? I need you to use words, shortie."

"Yes, Alex! A million times yes! In this life and the next, my little closeted hippie-dork," I shout next to his ear and he chuckles. *My favorite sound in the world.*

Alex grabs my hand and slides the most perfect ring I've ever seen onto my ring finger. The whole room breaks into a joyous laughter. In this moment, I realize that *this*—my people, all together in a room, with the man I love looking at me like I'm the greatest invention since chocolate—is the greatest gift. The gift rarely given that I get to have for the rest of my life.

DO you want to know who's Alex favorite romance author is? Read the bonus epilogue. Warning, it's spicy! You can find all my bonus epilogues at www.acordovabooks.com/playlists too!

Acknowledgments

-

HI!!

THANK you so much for reading this super fun and wild Christmas novella. I wrote this story because Alex and Livie wouldn't stop talking in my brain. They must have known how much I love the holiday season and how much I needed a fun and quick story. I hope you enjoyed it as much as I loved writing it.

I have so many people to say thank you to but I want to start with YOU because without your love for my stories and your support, I wouldn't be here. This story would probably not exist if it wasn't for you so thank you.

Thank you to my favorite and forever football player, Joey. There's always some of you in all of my main characters and that's no difference for this one either. Thank you for believing in me like a small child believes in Christmas—wholeheartedly.

Thank you to one of my readers, Gabi Ladd, for naming this novella. I had Alex and Livie's story stuck in my head for so long but afraid that the title wouldn't match the rest of the series, I asked for help from my ARC team. Gabi came up with the perfect name in like 10 seconds. This one's for you <3

To my alphas and betas, Mandy, Adriana, Kristina, Karen, Diane, and Colleen, thank you for always jumping into reading my work even when it's last minute and incomplete. I love you all.

To my author friends, Sarah, Rachel, Hailey, Hollie, Jenn, Allie, and Alexis, thank you for being my sanity when I decided to write a novella in two weeks. Thank you for the sprints and for the unconditional support. Thank you, Veronica, Emily, and Bella for continuing to be my moms in this journey. I would be so lost without you all. Double thanks to Veronica for letting me borrow a little bit of Iced Out for a bonus scene.

To my kids because you remind me to believe in magic again, every day. Thank you for your patience as mami navigates writing, working, and parenting.

To my editing team, Jayné and Kendra, what would I even do without you? I'd have a very, very, very unfinished manuscript for sure. These stories are what they are because of you. Love you!

To Kim from KBG Design and Mayhara from Mayharate for the most beautiful cover in the entire world. I'm forever obsessed with the two of you. You will never get rid of me, that's for sure.

To Cassie, I don't even know what to call you. My right hand? My sanity? My ultimate hype girl? I don't know what I would do without you and Cassie's Creative. Thank you. Thank you. Thank you.

To my street team. I love you all. That's all.

And last but not least, thank you to Joey again. Thank you for being my greatest gift.

Now, off to cry in author tears and on to the next book.
143,
Ambar

ABOUT THE AUTHOR

Ambar writes heartfelt, diverse, and emotional romance. Her stories are multicultural with a focus on raw storytelling and flawed characters who drive the plot forward with their challenges and growth. She has independently published four complete novels and two novellas, all featuring interracial couples with a range of dynamics. Her books are open-door romances that evoke tears, with high tension and delicious happily ever afters.

When Ambar is not writing she's chasing chickens or children, going on adventures with her family, crying over fictional people, dancing and reading in her she shed. Ambar enjoys boat rides, traveling, and spending time outside.

www.ingramcontent.com/pod-product-compliance
Lightning Source LLC
Chambersburg PA
CBHW020042310726

48970CB00007B/2373